bound to you

NEW YORK TIMES BESTSELLING AUTHOR

SHAWNTELLE MADISON

Praise for Shawntelle Madison

This deeply personal love story . . . has plenty of appeal thanks to sexual tension, second chances, and a marvelous central couple.

Publisher's Weekly

Shawntelle Madison creates sexual tension that practically burns the page. *Bound to You* is a must-read!

Mandy Baxter, author of the Billionaire's Club Series

An enjoyable read with a fun, flirty and budding romance.

Once Upon an Alpha

Definitely a keeper, I am quite looking forward to Sophie's friend Carlie's story, which is up next.

The Good, the Bad, and the Unread

Experiencing this journey with Sophie and Xavier is a treat. *Bound to You* is sweet, sexy, and funny, with a happily ever after that will touch your heart.

Cassie Ryan, author of My Obsession

First Printing: July 2018

ISBN-13: 978-0-9966701-4-2

ISBN-10: 0-9966701-4-9

eISBN-13: 978-0-9966701-5-9

Cover design: The Killion Group, Inc.

Chapter One

Sophie

W hen I first started working as a concierge for the rich and famous, my best friend Carlie gave me one valuable tip that I've never forgotten: *Everyone is hiding a fucking diva, Sophie. I don't care if it's Aunt Edna or Uncle Edmund. The crazy is waiting to come out.*

At first, I didn't believe it. Carlie could be cynical once in a while. I mean, c'mon. What about nice old ladies and those folks who waited in line patiently?

I learned real fast that the nicest people could turn into the most demanding customer if not appeased. Case in point, the client blowing up my cellphone as I raced to the airport.

"I needed those reservations five minutes ago, Ms. Ashton. My wife is expecting them." The smooth, male voice on my cellphone line had severed and burned my last nerve. Pawning him off on my assistant Jesse wasn't going to happen. I wasn't that cruel.

"I'm still working on getting you that executive suite,

Mr. Duvall." All the while I smiled as I spoke. Smiling keeps you from saying what you're *really* thinking. "The Stanley Cup playoff suites have been sold out for the past six months. It will take a miracle to get you in. Lucky for you, I've been known to work a miracle or two. Give me some time." I hung up and got back to the business at hand.

When it came to clients I offered the best high-class concierge services to be found in Boston, but I had one rule thanks to Carlie: no divas. Now, classifying someone as a diva could be considered subjective, but I've been in the business for two years now. That was long enough to learn a thing or two. Divas made crazy phone calls, and in particular, only a diva would ask me to meet them in the middle of a private airfield at the Logan International Airport.

Mr. Duvall was a kitten in comparison.

This new client's assistant had called me an hour ago. He seemed desperate and in a bind to get coverage for his employer. The poor man also sounded like death warmed over, but he'd said one word in particular: *please*. Multiple times, I might add, and he'd given me something rather hard for any business owner to refuse, a contract with a one and *many* zeros after it.

My cellphone vibrated from a text this time. The message came from my newest client: *are you coming, miss ashton?*

"I've met all kinds of people with money," Carlie had said when she first helped train me. *"There's always somebody sampling the nutjob pie. Just be prepared for the crazies and you'll do fine."* It was true. Out of every bunch there had to be an outlier. The guy who couldn't do what normal people did: meet at a hotel or go out for dinner like most clients.

Instead, this particular one wanted me to meet him right as he got off the jet.

Xavier Quinn.

If I took care of him well, this guy could make my career.

Getting past airport security was easy. The walk to the plane wasn't too bad either. For a busy Friday afternoon in May, there was just enough breeze off the bay to make the day pleasant. I didn't have to go far to reach the landing strip for the airfield where several private jets headed for the nearby hangar or taxied to one of the many runways. I spied a sleek jet waiting next to a silver Bentley. With a quick glance at my watch, I confirmed my late arrival. 4:10 to be exact.

Way to make a first impression, Sophie.

The cost itself for him to keep his plane and his car waiting here for me had to be astronomical, but if you had your face on *Wired* and *Esquire* magazine I guessed you could pull that off, too.

The four-door Bentley hummed, but no one was inside except for the driver. He noticed my approach and immediately got out.

"Miss Ashton," he asked.

"That would be me." I shook his hand. Even the poor driver was expecting me.

"Mr. Quinn is waiting inside the jet." He offered me the kind of expression you'd give someone who needed to be prepared for what was to come. "You should hurry," he advised.

I nodded, trying my best to head up the plane steps in my heels. The wind whipped my brown hair into my face, stuck to my lip-gloss, and made me wish I'd pulled my hair back into a ponytail. From the outside, the sleek plane was practical, but the inside boasted opulence. Leather seats, private LCD TVs for each passenger, and enough space for anyone to sleep comfortably.

A leggy stewardess cleaned up from the last flight service. Just one man sat in the back. My once bold steps slowed. My heartbeat sped up.

It was him.

Instead of waiting for me to come to him, he stood and walked toward the middle to meet me.

Mr. Quinn assessed me with light blue eyes and a spark ran down my spine. The hint of a smile touched the side of his face. He must've found my hesitation amusing. I'd seen his face on countless advertisements and news stories. In each picture he wore casual attire—jeans and a T-shirt. The cool tech company look. But today he wore a sleek suit that showed off his wide shoulders and trim waist.

What I found the most appealing were the sharp edges on his face. His nose was perfectly straight, while his cheeks were long, yet curved enough to make him appear youthful. Briefly his full lips, which were wonderfully sculpted, formed a straight line and his brow furrowed as if he saw something he didn't like.

He was crazy gorgeous, and he was here on serious business.

A part of me told myself not to be intimidated. I'd secured front row hockey tickets to Bruins games for Matt Damon, VIP seats for the Boston Philharmonic Orchestra for the mayor of San Diego. Yet as I strolled down the galley toward him all that confidence whittled away, leaving my palms wet and my mouth dry. The confident businesswoman flew off toward the Atlantic Ocean.

"You made it safely," was all he said. His smooth voice coursed through me.

"The traffic was atrocious," I managed. Somehow I pushed a smile on my face as I gathered my wits about me.

He was like any other client. *Just take care of him and this assignment will be done before you know it.*

"Boston can be that way, but there are shortcuts here and there." He cocked a half-grin.

"Depends on where my journey began." The smirk I wanted to give him was replaced with the curt smile I gave all my clients. "Are you ready to get started? According to Ian, we shouldn't waste time."

"Not so fast." I started to leave, but he caught my right arm, only to let me go just as quickly. But, in that brief moment, his firm grip and his assessing gaze made me almost gasp. When he'd touched me, warmth from his large hand had spread through my chiffon blouse. He was mere inches from the tightly bound leather cuff on my wrist, something I haven't used in awhile. How long had it been since someone had grabbed me aggressively like that? Two years. That was a long time. I rather missed it.

I could've moved, but my heels were firmly planted to floor.

My breath hitched. Up close, he smelled amazing, a rich leather cologne that made me want to run my nose along his collarbone. He had the kind of blond hair that looked good whether it was windblown or styled. My gaze drifted to his full lips. He was an attractive client, nothing more.

When he spoke, his kind expression became stern. So he was all business now. "Before we go any further we have a few ground rules we need to discuss."

I tried to back up, only to find my back against one of the seats.

"What are your ground rules, Mr. Quinn?" I took out my smartphone so I could take notes. And keep myself professional.

He quirked a grin that messed with my insides. "One, I

don't like to hear no for an answer unless there is a logical reason."

I almost laughed at that one. My phone vibrated again, but I ignored it.

"May I ask why?" I inquired.

"In the business I'm in, there are logical solutions to nearly every problem. Telling me no is like telling me you're giving up without trying."

I nodded. That was easy enough. "Next?"

"I expect you to give me one hundred and fifty percent effort."

"I do that for every client." My phone should've gone to voicemail, but it didn't. Instead of looking at my face, Mr. Quinn was checking out the vibrating phone in my hand. Not good.

"Yes, you *did* do that for every client," he said firmly. "Now, I'd like you to do that just for me."

"Now wait, I made it clear to Ian that I still have other clients to manage over the next few weeks." My assistant handled the lower hanging fruit. The big dogs needed attention.

He crossed his arms. "Please tell them your schedule is full. Especially whoever is trying to call you right now."

How I wish I could turn this thing off? "I'm accustomed to working with multiple clients and making sure all needs are met. How would you feel if you were one of my clients and I told you someone else said your schedule wasn't important enough?"

"I'd ask them to write a *bigger* check. Business is business."

"Not everyone thinks that way, Mr. Quinn."

"A lot more than you'd think do."

My phone vibrated again. Once I got a private

moment I planned to either jam my heel into the screen or permanently put it on silent. "I'm so sorry. Excuse me."

I turned away from him to quickly answer the phone. Mr. Duvall needed to stop act this way. Immediately. As quietly as possible, I explained to him that I needed the line to be clear if he wanted me to secure the executive suite for him. Once I had Mr. Quinn squared away, I planned to call my contact with the Bruins organization to see what could be done. Not much at this point, but I planned to try.

By the time I pasted a smile on my face and turned back toward Mr. Quinn, he had his cellphone in hand, waiting for me.

"Apologies," I said. Ugh, this was so embarrassing. "I have a client that needs—"

"Tell him Suite 5 is his."

"Excuse me?"

"I know the Bruins owner. We've played golf a few times. Since we're friends, I buy a suite during the playoffs every year."

I held back a laugh. "You know the owner?"

Just the very idea that he swam in those kinds of circles blew my mind. The team owner was a billionaire, a man listed as one of the richest people in Forbes magazine. And they played golf a *few* times. Just looking at him it was hard to believe he was a tech giant in his early thirties.

"He's a cool guy. The Bruins use my software at their corporate office." He walked around me, making sure to not brush against me, and headed for the exit as if what he'd done was nothing.

When I didn't keep up, he threw words over his shoulder. "Are you coming, Miss Ashton?"

Chapter Two

Sophie

By the time we settled into the Bentley's leather backseat, I found a moment to murmur, "Thanks." If I weren't on the clock, I'd sigh from how comfortable everything felt. The car smelled divine. Almost as if the vehicle was meticulously cleaned or was rarely used. A guy like Quinn probably had a new car for every day of the week.

The need to glance at my phone nagged at me a bit, especially with a client like Mr. Duvall, but the moment my fingertip touched the screen, Mr. Quinn's side-glance made me freeze. I'd added as much space as possible between us, but he still seemed too close.

"Like I said," his voice was smooth, "I don't mind sharing my suite, but sharing my assistant isn't something I'm willing to do."

Well, I'd have to find a way to convince him otherwise. I had too many clients and even though I was grateful to him, I couldn't just abandon everyone for one client. No matter how well he paid.

The drive into the city was quiet. Too quiet for my taste. The need to turn my head left grew. Was he watching me? Did I even want to turn my head to find out? As the airport disappeared and the skyline grew, apprehension nipped at me. Time to go over what I learned from his assistant. "Ian told me you have a brief period of time to secure an important contract?"

Xavier nodded. "I have two weeks. I'm here for one man. A stubborn one. My company needs Nakamura Industries to develop a prototype based on ideas we've developed. Our projections show the profitability margin is very favorable, yet Hideo Nakamura has turned down my army of lawyers at Silver Sparrow Systems five times. Each reason was the same: lack of management credibility."

That surprised me. Over the past year, Xavier's company had been mentioned as one of the cutting edge outliers for mobile phone engineering.

"So he believes you're not good enough to work with him," I said.

"He's denied partnership to a few others, but he's got the people though to bring my ideas from concept to completion. Three other startup companies were interested in using Nakamura's facilities, but he turned them down. He comes from the old guard—traditionalists who see startups as failure points."

"If he's already turned you down, why bother trying?"

"Like I said before, I don't take no for an answer unless there is a logical reason." He appeared thoughtful for a moment. "Nakamura is in town to visit relatives and conduct business. I've tried elaborate backdoor tactics to get that man's attention, but I'm thinking what's left is the face-to-face approach. That is why you're here, Miss

Ashton. To get me that face-to-face. When we get to my vacation house, you can tell me how you plan to do that."

Rush hour slowed us down, but eventually we reached the affluent Back Bay neighborhood along Storrow Drive. Rows of Victorian brown houses lined the street. This was one of my favorite places to visit when I moved here from New York City. Especially since I had far less spectacular digs east of here in Orient Heights.

As we pulled into a private parking space along Beacon Avenue, I had a feeling a new game plan would be in order. Especially if he wanted to impress Nakamura. The location boasted wealth, but it wasn't ideal if we wanted to seize any opportunity that came up.

The driver opened the door for us and I followed him to the private elevator. From there we rode up to a penthouse with high ceilings, large windows, and hardwood floors. The last time I'd seen a home like this was on the cover of *Architectural Digest*.

Technology touched everything from the multi-screen security panel, to the lights that automatically lit as we entered what had to be Xavier's study. Voice-activated computer monitors, a desk, and countless bookshelves filled the far end. He picked up the stack of envelopes on the desk, scanned them, and quickly tossed them back shortly after.

"We need to get started on Nakamura." The way he focused on me was unnerving.

I nodded.

"Your home is amazing," I managed to say. This was the first time I'd visited a client's place, vacation home, or otherwise. For the kind of work I did, a phone call, fax, or an email did the job. Face-to-face communication wasn't as valuable anymore.

"Thanks. Acquiring property outside of Phoenix was

one of the first things I did once I made some money. A friend sold me the fifth floor since he didn't use it often enough."

My hand tightened on my purse. *Some money. That's an understatement.* He had the *whole* floor to himself. My apartment could fit in the corner.

I ran my fingers along the edge of a dark wooden computer desk. Not a single blemish. "Nakamura is here to visit family and conduct business, correct?"

He nodded and I hoped he took the news I was about to dropkick into his lap well.

"Then this place isn't ideal for your base of operations."

Xavier chuckled. "Should I tell you who my neighbors are downstairs? The basketball player on the ground level?"

"I'm sure they're great, but if you want Nakamura, you're gonna have to trust me on this decision."

He stared at me for a bit, his jaw twitching. He'd have to leave behind a few luxuries, but the sacrifice would be worth it once my plan was set in motion.

"Trust me," I added.

"And what would you suggest, then?"

Ten minutes later I was the one doing the leading—into a *much* smaller studio apartment in a tower building in downtown Boston. I held my breath, hoping he'd agree to the new location: Chinatown.

"It's not as large," I quickly said as he took in the single, two-level studio apartment, "but they have concierge service, security, a pool, and a fully-equipped training facility."

He strolled through the living room. There wasn't much to it—a couch, a TV, and a computer desk. "I haven't lived in a room this small since college," he joked.

I hadn't gone to a traditional university so I couldn't relate, but I had an idea what he meant. To me the apartment was roomy, yet cozy, with brick walls and stainless steel appliances. Just the kind of place for a bachelor on the rise.

"Why here?" he asked smoothly. Every time he walked past me, with his arms crossed and his amused expression, I couldn't shake the rising tension in my stomach. He was like a circling shark and I was prey. Was he like this with everyone?

My fingertips traced the line along the edge of my wrist strap for reassurance. I walked to the northern window and pulled back the curtains. The evening Boston skyline opened up to us and I pointed to a tiny building nestled between an office and a restaurant. "That is the reason."

He joined me. "I've never been there before. What is it?"

"I've yet to have a client visiting from Japan who doesn't consider bringing their business associates there for entertaining. It's Sakura No Hana. A traditional Japanese tea house." He continued to stare at the teahouse and the hints of a handsome smile touched his lips as I spoke again. "Matter of fact, most of my clients request accommodations at the Ritz-Carlton—which is a block away. I can do some digging, and by morning, I should be able to figure out where Nakamura is staying—"

"He's at the Ritz," Xavier supplied.

I couldn't hide my triumphant smile that time.

Way to go, Sophie!

He turned to nod at me, and I fell into his light blue eyes. He was just at the right height for me to look at his lips. To take in how they parted. Damn. "Very nice," he said.

He meant the arrangements, right?

I broke the moment before I said something foolish. "If you want Nakamura, you should be as close to him as possible. We also need to show him you're serious—not hanging out in your playboy penthouse." I almost wished I could've snatched those last words back, but he immediately answered.

"I agree."

"Great." My cheeks filled with heat as I sighed. Things had progressed well so far. "Let me check a few restaurants like Shojo, Classica, or maybe even Da Vinci Ristorante to see what I can shake up. Maybe a manager can find reservations under his name."

While he browsed through the studio, I made a few phone calls to the popular spots and five-star restaurants. Touched base with a good friend named Tony who owned three major establishments in town. I scratched their backs with affluent customers and they hooked me up in return. Once I had the information I needed, I found Xavier upstairs in the bedroom loft.

Right next to the massive king-size bed.

There wasn't room for much else on the loft level. The bed had a thick, mahogany headboard. The sturdy posts drew my eyes, so I quickly looked away.

He leaned on the balcony rail near the end table. "What did you find out?"

What immediately came to mind was the fact I didn't want to imagine my client on or near his bed. I didn't see him perched on the end, leaning forward with his elbows resting on his knees, a look of hunger in his eyes. And, most importantly, I didn't hear him telling me, *"Lay down right there. Raise your arms so I can tie you to the bed."*

My imagination was running rampant today. I barely

knew this man, yet the idea of being trapped under his hard stare made my thighs clench tight with need.

I cleared my throat. "You'll be having dinner tonight at Classica. Nakamura's party has reservations for seven sharp."

He took a step toward me, his gaze never leaving mine.

I took one step down the stairs. Hanging out in the bedroom of a client, in particular one who was infamous for his many entanglements with supermodels, actresses, and other celebrity eye candy, was not wise.

"Now that your dinner arrangements are in order, I'll leave you to your evening." I took another step, my hand tightening on the railing. "Will that be all?"

He strolled over to me. Confident. Assured. I took a step backward. It was time for me to go. Now.

"Not in the least," he said firmly. "You're not off the clock yet."

Chapter Three

Xavier

Just one long look at the woman in front of me and I knew there was no way in hell I was letting Sophie leave my side tonight.

The flushed skin along her collarbone drew my eye. She held onto the railing as if it were the only thing holding her up. Her hazel eyes blinked at me, her glossy pink lips parting for her tongue to slip out and lick the bottom lip. Damn. She had it all. A small waist. The kind of clingy black skirt that made a man want to run his hands along the curves to the hem and drag it up to see if she wore garters underneath it. The woman was practically delicious.

"How do you know I don't have plans tonight?" She sized me up with a straight face.

"You do have them," I said coolly. "With me."

I took another step closer to her and she stiffened. With one misstep she'd break her neck falling down those goddamn steps. "Whoa there. I'm not comfortable with you standing there," I said. "It's a long way down." I raised my hands in surrender. "I promise I don't bite. I'm more of a nibbler."

Sophie laughed, her beautiful face lighting up as she took tentative steps up the stairs to join me. Her professional visage faded again for a moment and I welcomed the change. She left as much distance as she could between us and found a spot near the only dresser in the room. "See? Safe and sound."

I nodded. "Thanks—now to the business at hand, namely how I hired you to take care of me."

She pursed her lips. "Ian said to take care of all your needs, but the contract he sent me said nothing about accompanying you *everywhere*."

"Well, then I'm sure he told you I'm willing to do anything to secure this contract and your services were acquired to make that happen. Unless you need to save the world, you need to come up with a good reason why you can't help me tonight."

Like a family. Or perhaps another client I needed to silence.

A small smile formed on her lips. She crossed her arms as if she chewed on the idea of giving in. I never accepted no unless the answer was reasonable—and as of right now Sophie hadn't given me a good one.

Before my jet had landed I'd expected to find a stiff matronly woman waiting for me. Ian's sense of humor was dry like that. But when Sophie walked onto the plane, a sinking feeling came over me.

With a beautiful woman at my side, I'd have a lot more distractions other than my company, Nakamura, and the contract during this trip. She'd sauntered down the aisle, in black heels and a tight pencil skirt, her shoulder-length, brown hair in layers around her face. She was just another hired employee until she'd opened her mouth and showed me she could think fast on her feet.

I instantly liked her.

Which I now see was a poor decision on my part.

There was a reason why I employed men like Ian for my personal assistant needs. After my girlfriend Rosalie's death five years ago, the idea of having a woman close to me in any capacity wasn't welcomed. Unless they wanted to *play*—but Miss Ashton was my employee and I've never revealed my sexual proclivities to my employees. My kinky lifestyle was none of their business.

Sophie still hadn't answered me and I held back my amusement. There was something about her that intrigued me: maybe it was her hesitation. Most of my employees reacted too quickly, answering questions without thought as if such an action would impress me.

I did want to know what she was thinking though.

"Dinner and nothing else other than getting you settled into the apartment," she finally said. "No fraternizing. No drinks afterward."

Good try. Not good enough. "If Nakamura is still conducting business after dinner, then we'll have to reassess that decision."

I was here on business, wasn't I?

Her gaze flicked to the bed and then back to me. As much as I'd like to see her on top of it, we had less than an hour to get to Classica.

"Why do you keep looking at the bed?" I asked.

"It's rather hard to miss." She sucked in a breath. "I wonder how they got the bed post up here. The wood looks pretty heavy and thick."

"A few burly guys. Some pizzas and beer afterwards." I ran my right hand over the blood-red bedspread, then the smooth bedpost. Sophie had good taste. "It's rather nice. Did you personally pick out this unit for me?"

"No…But do you like it?" Her smile was gone, but even the playful undertones to the question made me hard as hell.

"I can work with it—but I'll need my desktop and monitors delivered from the house on Beacon." My voice came out thick. We'd just met and she was already messing with me.

"I've got a few technicians on speed-dial who can take care of those details." She headed for the stairwell and I followed her. I couldn't help but watch the way her clothes slid over her skin as she walked. "By the time you return tonight, your studio will be fully stocked with everything you need during your trip."

DOWNTOWN BOSTON at night awaited us. I'd forgotten how much I enjoyed the vibe. I only got to briefly take in downtown before we got into the Bentley, but one glance was enough: pedestrians traffic along the sidewalks, back-to-back cars honking along the street. *And the good smells.* If I was younger—and not as busy—I'd be tempted later tonight to head down to Washington Street to the rows of smaller, trendy restaurants.

But, I wasn't as young, and I had no time to explore.

Our short drive west to Back Bay was a silent one, but we'd be talking soon enough.

Classica was elegant eatery off Bolyston Street. As expected around dinnertime, the restaurant was packed. I never had to work hard to get into a restaurant with my status, but this time I hung back and waited to see what she could do.

As hard as I tried not to let my mind wander in that direction, I still couldn't help seeing how much Sophie reminded me of Rosalie. Not in appearance, mind you, but they both had similar height and Rosalie's hair was light blonde versus Sophie's brown hair. What seemed to differ between them was *how* they hustled. If something needed to be done, Rosalie handled the matter promptly, but always with that cold demeanor of hers. Before I'd met her, she had been one of the top financial advisors in Los Angeles. With a single phone call, her clients made millions. She had an uncanny way of analyzing markets to find opportunities. Even if those opportunities would *appear* underhanded to others. To her the world was an ocean that constantly ebbed and flowed. You had to adapt for the right moment—and that meant closing off yourself to others who might stand in the way of that goal. They were two different women, yet they did the same thing: Rosalie studied markets to make money for her clients while Sophie studied people to do the same.

Maybe that was why I found Sophie so fascinating. I always had a thing for women who knew how to get what they wanted.

Sophie leaned in to whisper to the maitre'd once we arrived. He immediately nodded. She had secured us a spot beforehand. She was that good. I scanned the room as we walked to the table. Classica was a cozy Italian restaurant with standard dark blue decor and Mediterranean rustic feel. If you've been to one restaurant, you'd been to them all, but it was the food that piqued my interest. Every customer enjoyed his or her food and the wine flowed freely. That was my kind of place. Empty plates meant good food.

We reached our table, a two-seater. Sophie tried to sit, but I reached in and pulled her chair out for her. As I pushed her forward I caught a brief scent of her hair. Intoxicating. Her hair was thick and flowed down her back. Almost begging for me to run my fingers through it. "It may not seem like it, but I do appreciate you coming," I whispered.

"Appreciate?" She tried to hold back a smile, but wasn't doing too good of a job. "Coerced is more like it."

The waiter handed us our menus. "When was the last time you ate?" I asked her.

"I had a power bar for lunch and then the phone calls began," she admitted as she looked over her menu.

Meanwhile, a party to my far right caught my eye. Nakamura and four other men laughed and enjoyed a meal at a corner table. We had a great vantage point.

"Would you like anything from our wine list?" our waiter asked.

I didn't bother looking. I wasn't much of a wine guy, but I drank it on occasion. Give me a beer and I'd be fine. Late night coding didn't go well with wine.

"Anything you want?" I asked her. I asked for an imported beer. The menu obscured part of her face, but I caught her hazel eyes and the perfect arcs of her eyebrows. From what I could see her face was almost symmetrical. Practically perfect compared to most. Her long eyelashes blinked and I almost missed what wine she recommended.

"That sounds fine," I said.

We gave our orders and then sat in silence until Sophie spoke.

"Have you found him yet?" she asked. Already onto business.

"Of course, but I'm not concerned about him right now." I leaned back. Now that the menu was gone, I had an unobstructed view of my new assistant.

"You should be. He's meeting with Hayato Takahashi

and Kaito Watanabe. They are pretty big hitters in the technology field."

So she knew who they were. Interesting. Her voice became lyrical, almost musical when she pronounced their names. Like she knew Japanese. She tried to get me to look at them, but I didn't bother to follow her gaze. They weren't going anywhere anytime soon and just knowing Takahashi and Watanabe were here told me my target was open to discussing business. If his dinner tonight were only personal he wouldn't be entertaining others in the tech field.

"I know who they are," I said. "What I want to know is your plan of attack this week."

She shrugged. Her phone buzzed and she turned it off with an annoyed expression. Good. Now I had her complete attention. The waiter brought the wine and then poured each of us a glass. He gave me a Dutch beer, too. Once we sampled the wine and approved it, he left the bottle.

"As much as I'd like to plan things to the minute, I have a feeling you'll need to be prepared for anything. A last minute wine tasting trip, a drive to the countryside. Of course Nakamura's staff wouldn't disclose his schedule during his stay, so I put a private detective on his trail. Nothing too obvious, but we need someone to track him and I'm in no position to creep around in the middle of the night in a catsuit."

"You'd look good though. Are you sure you don't want to hide behind garbage cans and sneak around? You could add spy to your resume." I cocked a grin.

"Not happening." She returned a small smile.

"You hired a PI? Not a move I'd make, but I can work with that." She was clever. I liked that.

Our meals arrived, a grilled tenderloin for me and a

pan-roasted halibut for her, but neither of us really ate much. I couldn't help admiring her face as I took a slow swig of my beer. The brew went down smooth.

"What?" She caught me looking and touched her hair-line. "Do I have something weird on my face or something?"

"Nope. I'm curious about something, though. Ian wouldn't hire just anyone, but I've never heard of you before. And I've been to Boston a few times."

"So you want my story." She licked her lips and I wanted to taste the red wine that lingered there. Let the dry taste slide over my tongue.

"Whatever you're willing to share," I managed. "You've already seen where I'm sleeping tonight. The least you can do is convince me you won't sneak into my room and do me in."

Her eyes sparked mischievously. "I'm not the sneak-in type. If I'm gonna eliminate a problem, I have people I call."

"Oh, so it's like that."

She had a lively laugh. "Yes, it is."

"How long have you been in business?"

"Over two years. It occupies all of my time."

I played with my beer bottle, then glanced at her hand. She didn't wear a ring. "A beautiful woman like you should have some fun once in a while. Maybe even get a boyfriend."

"How do you know I don't have a boyfriend?"

"I don't." I paused. "Do you?"

"No, I don't and no, I don't date my clients," she said, keeping her voice even. The phrase came fast as if she'd said it many times before.

I chuckled. "I didn't say anything about dating. Miss

Ashton, flirting with a woman who has a boyfriend isn't my style—"

She leaned forward, trying to keep her voice low. "Did you miss what I said?"

"I heard what you said, Miss Ashton. Look, I'm not trying to start anything serious either. For the past five years, I haven't been interested in anything serious for personal reasons. A girlfriend is the last thing I'm looking for—but that doesn't mean I wouldn't like to enjoy an evening out with a gorgeous woman."

She stiffened, apparently taken aback.

"Am I allowed to have dinner with a beautiful woman?" I repeated.

She gestured around us. "There are plenty of beautiful women." Her eyes darkened. "There are even escort services, too. I've made that type of call before if you need it."

Now that was an attempt at a low blow, but I was ready for it. "If I wanted an escort tonight, I could've called an old friend or two. The conversation and company wouldn't have been as interesting, though. I want to be with you tonight."

Her mouth opened with a retort, but nothing came out.

Our gazes locked and we stared at each other for a moment. It was true, I could've called a number of past flings who would've jumped at the opportunity to play out a scene or two, but I wanted Sophie. She was here for business only—she wasn't flirting with me or jumping at the chance to see if I was looking for the next Mrs. Quinn to take to my huge family affairs. That alone was refreshing and made it far too easy for me to say what I wanted.

She bit her lower lip and shifted in her seat. As she ran

her right hand through her thick hair, the scent of her sweet perfume reached me and jumped straight to my cock. My imagination went wild, picturing her straddling my lap. Just the thought of grabbing a fistful of her locks to force her to arch her long back made my throat go dry. She would be beautiful, completely inhibited as she rode my lap.

The ambience around us faded until there was nothing left but me and her.

"I'm gonna be honest here," I said slowly. "The minute I saw you step on the plane, I wanted someone else. I'm not here for fun. But then you stepped up your game, and now I'm glad you're on my team. I'd like to see what other things you're good at, too."

"That's it?" Her voice was breathy as she issued her challenge.

I chuckled. There was a lot more. "Every time you run your hands through your hair, I've wanted to grab it, bend you over your seat, and fuck you senseless."

There. I said it.

With her left hand's ring finger she ran the fingertip along a line of exposed black leather, peeking out from her blouse circling on her right wrist. When she caught me looking, she quickly pulled the sleeve over it. I clenched my fist to keep myself from snaking my hand out to catch her wrist.

"That's not for you," she said, her eyes following where my gaze lay.

"What is it?"

She gave me a small smile. "Let's straighten things out between me and you, Mr. Quinn. I'm probably not like the last woman you dated. Not even close. I prefer not to reveal my private life to others. Especially the kinky things I do in my own bed. I'm sorry, but I won't be doing that kind of thing in yours."

A pleasurable shudder flowed through me and my fist tightened. I'd only caught a brief glimpse of what she wore on her wrist, but I could almost imagine running my thumb along the smooth material, then stroking the skin along the edge. As much as I was getting turned on, I had to careful though. Maybe she belonged to another Dominant.

Our gazes locked. Her confident smile faded. Her lips parted and her gaze grew heated.

I waited for her to say something. To tell me to fuck off. But she said nothing, only watching me as her breasts rose and fell with her rapid breaths.

Finally, she looked away. She had to know she'd issued a challenge and I rarely backed down from one once it was set before me.

She stirred what was left of her halibut around her plate. Neither of us seemed interested in our food anymore.

Someone moved to my right. Nakamura and his friends had completed their meal and gotten up to leave. There was nothing holding us here anymore. Another opportunity might come soon. I was just as tenacious as Miss Ashton.

My tongue was thick in my mouth when I finally spoke. "It looks like Nakamura is done for the night so we should go. I'd like to give you a ride home, Miss Ashton." Among other things.

Her fingertips slipped down her wine glass flute and then back up. The subtle motion kicked me below the belt.

She slid out of her seat, her gaze never leaving mine. "I'd like that ride, Mr. Quinn."

❧

Sophie

Carlie, who just made a job offer last week for me to relocate to London, would probably tell me I was making a mistake. That a man like Xavier Quinn should be rode into the sunset. Even I had to admit I was tempted. Keyword *tempted*.

Neither of us spoke as we left the restaurant, but once we reached the sidewalk I had to say something.

"Do you need my address?" I asked.

He didn't answer until the Bentley pulled up and Chris opened the door.

"Get inside," was all he said.

A quiver raced down my spine. There was a push behind his words that time. I quickly got in. It had been two years since someone had moved me like that, but now wasn't the time to think about my ex-boyfriend Sato. He was long gone overseas.

All sorts of clients have tried to get into my pants before. They used all kinds of pick up lines or assumed that as the hired help I was also the hired whore.

But tonight was different.

There was something about the way he took charge when he spoke. I had outright told him I wasn't interested. We had just met and he was a client. Yet on the inside I yearned for him to touch me like he did on the airplane. To grab my hips with his large hands like he gripped my wrist. To see his light blue eyes grow intense every time he stared at me.

And he was a virtual stranger, no less.

I slipped into the Bentley. The driver asked for my address and I quickly supplied the information for East Boston. All the while, I remained on my side of the car trying not to think about him. The dinner's events all too fresh in my mind. As we sat there, not eating, tension stretched from limb to limb, making it harder for me to ignore the obvious: I couldn't work for him like this. Working day-to-day with a man who had told me he wanted to fuck me senseless. Every time I'd see him I'd know. I'd remember his words and that particular conversation would make it damn near impossible for me to do my job.

And just the thought of getting the sexual tension out of the way was difficult to resist. We could go back to his studio apartment, we'd do what needed to be done, and then tomorrow I'd be fine. An itch scratched. A hunger sated. No promises for something more.

By the time we pulled up to my brick apartment building in Orient Heights, I managed to find some of the control I'd lost. Less than a foot separated us, but he didn't move thank goodness.

Silence folded over us and all I could do was face forward. The still air in the car grew heavy. The weight of his gaze intensified.

"I'll see you bright and early tomorrow morning, Miss Ashton. Sleep well."

"Bright and early."

As I walked up to the building, my confidence strengthened. He was nothing more than an attractive client. Losing everything I'd gained was unacceptable.

Chapter Four

Sophie

As expected, the living room lights cast a bright glow through the large bay window in my second-story apartment. By the time I walked through the door, I wasn't surprised to see Lana, one of my two roommates, with her papers and books scattered all over what little space we had.

I stepped over *Netter's Atlas of Human Anatomy* and leaped over a bunch of drawings of body parts most folks didn't want to see. Was that a left arm? Or maybe a dissected upper thigh? Yep, ignorance was bliss.

"You're back early," Lana remarked. The short, redhead never looked up. As usual, she was wearing an alternative rock band T-shirt. This time it was *Modest Mouse*. Ever since her first-year second semester started at U Mass, I only saw the back of her head most of the time. My other roommate, Penny, was home far more than I preferred due to her work-from-home gig. Like Carlie, I grew up with Penny in the foster care system in NYC. Compared to sharing a room in foster care with Carlie, who never picked up her belongings unless they were on fire, Penny was a much tidier roommate.

"I had an uneventful night." Now that was an understatement. Just thinking about Xavier made my brain tumble. My cellphone buzzed in my pocket as I left the living room walking toward the bedrooms. The three-bedroom apartment wasn't that big, but with one medical student and a phone-sex operator paying part of the bills, the place was much more affordable.

Since I'd lived here first, I offered to give Lana the biggest bedroom so she could have a study nook, but she declined.

"You won't see me here half the time," Lana had said when we'd first made the agreement. "If I get comfortable, I'm sleeping," she had added. "My scholarship only goes so far in helping me not get screwed over by the crazy-high tuition costs. I should be at the library, in class, or sleeping in that bed."

In a way, I was rather glad. The amount of clothes and stuff I had were astronomical. I might've been only a concierge, but for the kind of business I was in, I had to be flexible in terms of my attire.

I thought she was engrossed in her homework, but she eagerly followed me into the narrow galley kitchen. "You're never home this early," Lana said as she grabbed a Coke after I got my bottle of water. "I've been wondering if something is up."

"So I gather," I said dryly.

"All you do is work and come home late." She took a long sip of her drink. "When it comes to dating, Penny and I never hear you talk about anyone." She said this as if she wished she had a date.

"Do you seriously want me bringing a guy here when

you're studying?" She flashed me a look as if I'd fallen down the steps on the way up to the apartment.

"I've never had a drought like this since high school," she said. "Even the guys in the second-year class look tired and broke down. I wish our professors weren't so good looking."

She hopped on the kitchen counter and propped her feet up on the other side, effectively barring my escape. "Sophie, there's a professor in the internal medicine department that has 'fuck me please' written across his forehead," she said in a rapid burst. "We need to get you two together somehow."

Any time the wind blew, Lana had a new crush. The poor woman had made a vow of celibacy for her first year, focusing on her studies foremost, and now she was trying to hook me up with every dude she came across.

"The guy has an amazing body!" The look of lust was all over her face. "I accidentally bumped into him on the way to the gross lab and his abs…" She shuddered with delight. "I could tongue-surf my way down to his lollipop garden."

I almost choked on my water.

"I wanna tongue-surf somebody someday," she added with a sigh.

As much as I appreciated Lana's efforts, none of the guys who tried to hit on me really did anything for me. Just because a man was attractive, didn't mean he had everything I needed. And don't get me started on the guys who pretended they had a dominant side to them.

They'd say, "You like it rough, dontcha, babe…" *No, not really.*

Men who have a dominant nature are born that way. They exude it, and so far, the men who have lined up to play on my playground couldn't swing that way even if they tried.

After listening to Lana describe every enticing feature Dr. Hanley had, I ambled into my room, toed off my heels and discarded my purse in the corner.

She briefly poked her head into the room. "You got another package from overseas. I left it on your bed. Penny tried to open it, but I managed to hide it before she used a box cutter. Looks like something expensive."

My chest tightened. I didn't dare look at the pretty white box. Or my name written in neat cursive on the label. For the last two years, a new package arrived every couple of months from the same address in Japan. I used to throw them away, not caring if they contained apologies, expensive presents, or pleas. Right now I didn't feel like dealing with the ghosts of past boyfriends, so I placed the package in a neat spot elsewhere.

My phone buzzed with a message, but I ignored it. Keeping my professional life out of my personal one was impossible at times.

You know you're going to check it in about two minutes... Yeah, I was gonna check it, but I preferred to think that I was capable of waiting a bit and not responding immediately.

What if it's him?

Him, as in Xavier Quinn, who should either be sleeping right now to prepare for tomorrow or doing work for his company.

I glanced at my purse where I'd left my phone. *Not gonna check it.* It was probably that guy who wanted boxed seats. He probably wanted a chance to meet the owner, too. My thoughts immediately drifted to dinner as I unzipped the back of my skirt and let the garment fall to the floor. I stepped out and headed to my bed. My gaze swept over my bed.

If you really wanted he could've been in this bed tonight, I thought. *You could've been making loud noises and giving your roommates a real anatomy education.* A sex education. I did have a queen-sized bed. It was nothing compared to the monstrous king-sized bed in Xavier's room. My iron bedpost was just as sturdy as his, but not as expensive and intricate. Was he in bed right now? I shook my head and sat on the mattress which was warm and comforting. Almost beckoning me to do what I always did when I was alone and longed for company. Release could be found overnight, curled up on my side with my hands stretched out in front of me bound at the wrists. Memories from the exquisite tight sensation stretched up my arms and settled into my stomach. I hummed with delight. All I had to do was open my locked bedside drawer. My wrists itched and I rubbed the skin under my leather cuffs.

My phone buzzed again. I still hadn't checked the pending message.

Check the phone, you fool. It was probably not him anyway. *Remember you're running a business*, I reminded myself.

I retrieved my phone. I'd make this quick.

I had one single message. The number and the name was new, but familiar now.

I backed up to the bed and sat.

"Are you up?" the message read.

My fingers hovered over the keypad. He had no business messaging me right now. I took a deep breath. This was easy to handle.

"It's only nine, Mr. Quinn."

I moved to put the phone down, but the response was lightning fast. What was he doing?

"So what's on the agenda for tomorrow?" he wrote.

"I'll send you an email early in the morning with our plans."

The reply appeared. *"Nothing else tonight?"*

My breath skittered and my thigh muscles clenched. No, nothing else tonight. Even as tempted as I might be.

"There's nothing to discuss yet," I quickly typed. My brain lost focus for a moment. This part should be easy. Just tell him to watch a pay-per-view fight or a flick on Netflix and call it a day. *"We..."* And then I had nothing.

"We..." he began. *"We what?"*

My finger hovered over the G key. There were so many things I could say. That we're going to whatever event the PI determined would be best. That we should have a breakfast meeting—in public—to go over a plan of attack.

The phone rang. He was trying to call me. By the third ring I finally gave in and picked up.

"Is everything all right, Ms. Ashton?" He had amusement in his voice. The casual timbre of someone who was relaxed. My imagination ran amuck, feeding me an image of him sitting in his tiny bachelor apartment; propped up in a chair with his shirt slightly open...

"Miss Ashton?"

"Everything's fine. It's been a long day with clients and I haven't had any down time all day."

"You did mention during dinner that you'd only had a protein bar. Should I be concerned you won't be up for the rigorous work I had in mind?"

I didn't miss the double entendre in his words and I tried to let them skim off my back. "I'll keep up just fine. I'd say you should be the one ready for what comes up. We might be changing plans on the fly so I'd be prepared for anything from golf matches to the opera. Pretty much anything."

Now that I was talking business the tension in my stomach melted a bit. This was the Sophie I depended on. The confident person.

"Sounds good." He grew quiet. Any moment now I

expected him to hang up. In the silence I waited to hear the sounds of a television, the hum of something else.

"Is there anything else you need, Mr. Quinn?" I held my breath. Would he say what he had been thinking during dinner? That he wanted to fuck me? That our evening wasn't over yet?

I detected his smile. Or maybe I thought he was smiling. The brief clink of someone drinking from a shot glass. "As of right now, there are many things I *need*, but tomorrow is a new day. Good night, Miss Ashton." The click and then I was left sitting there like a fool.

I connected my phone to the charger and got to work at my desk. There were things to tackle and little time to do them. But as the night stretched along, my gaze kept flicking to the drawer next to my bed. The hunger that filled me all evening had left my stomach gathered in uncomfortable knots.

Reluctantly casting my work aside, I went to the drawer and unlocked it. Scattered among my ropes, gathered in neat bundles, I spied a single handwritten note.

A note I should've thrown away a long time ago, but I clung to Sato's goodbye note, or maybe I should say it still clung to me.

Chapter Five

Sophie

As expected, my bed didn't bring any comfort. Every direction I lay seemed like an exercise in futility. By the time I settled upside down with my pillow under my feet, the clock read two-thirty A.M.

Lovely.

Unfortunately, for me I still considered two a perfect good time to work. From birth I never slept more than a few hours.

And with time to burn I became pensive and restless. And when I got pensive I thought about the past. Beside me, my bedside drawer was shut. I was determined to keep its contents locked away. I even put on the most obnoxious light green pajamas as proof that I had no desire to go there. To let my mind wander until I sought out comfort.

And yet, going there happened.

My fingers reached out to the bedpost at the foot of the bed near my head. The metal was warm and the scratches along the bar whispered secrets of past pleasures. On a night like tonight two years ago, I had waited in this very bed for Sato, cellphone in hand, and fear in chest. Fear due to the fact that he had sent me a text message in the afternoon that had read: *Something important to tell you. Be ready at 8.*

Which in "Sato-language" meant to expect him at 7:55 pm. He had the punctuality of dawn. Always expected at the scheduled time.

But he didn't show up as expected.

Sato had hinted over the past week that his father wanted him to return to Nagasaki for a family gathering. After he had worked for so long as an intern for a local tech company, Sato deserved a vacation.

Tonight might be the night he asks me to go to Japan with him.

Eight o'clock came and went. All I had was the silence in the apartment and my worries. Had he gotten hurt? Was he unconscious in a hospital somewhere? None of my phone calls to his friends led anywhere.

By the time it was 10 p.m., I turned off my bedside lamp and stretched out onto the mattress. The sheets cooled my warm skin, yet sleep eluded me. What the hell was I doing staying here? Shouldn't I go out and look for him? But I knew not to.

Because I always followed his orders.

When my boyfriend made a request, I complied. I wanted to. To lay there patiently until he joined me in bed. That was one of my kinks and he sated my hunger whenever he could.

More time passed and finally I heard the front door to my apartment opening and closing.

Soon enough, fingertips brushed against my ankle as sleep weighed heavy on my eyelids. Then a warm hand grasped the pad of my foot.

A smile touched my lips. Sato always had a thing for feet.

"You have the feet of a China doll," he'd once said. *"A bit bigger than my stretched out palm."*

He caressed my thighs, then my hips as he trailed his way upwards. Then the warmth of his naked body covered mine. I ran my nose along his chest, my breath drawing in his intoxicating spicy citrus scent. He was all lean muscle. Wiry, yet strong. In the darkness, I could only make out faint shadows, but Sato's face was visible in my mind. Every hard line. Every feature I'd memorized since we began seeing each other a little over a year ago.

I opened my mouth to express my concern, but immediately tossed the idea aside when he gently tugged my arm toward the top of the bed. My right hand first. Then the left. Anticipation made my breath catch. And oh, what a wonderful stretch I felt along my limbs as he fastened the O-links on my leather wrist cuffs to the short chains attached to the bedpost.

Afterward, his lips trailed from one of my nipples to the other one. Soft, brief caresses. He lingered long enough to thrill me, yet leave me lusting for more.

He checked my restraints to make sure they weren't too tight. Everything was nice and snug. I was completely secure. Once, he'd watched me all night like this, making me wait until I was soaking wet and squirming under his gaze. It was all about the anticipation. The moment when he'd finally touch me and I'd climax from a single stroke to my clit.

Tonight he didn't hold back. Perhaps this was my reward after waiting so long. Sato gripped my hips to hold me in place while his tongue followed the curve of my thigh. Each swirl he made was slow and sensual until he shifted me to dip his tongue into my belly button. When his head lowered even further to French kiss my clit, I had to swallow the moan circling the back of my throat.

There was nowhere he didn't touch. The nape of my neck. The ticklish skin along the crack of my ass. The tips of my breasts that begged for his lips. Every inch of me sang from his nibbles, bites, and sucks.

He plucked orgasms from me like a virtuoso played a concerto on a violin. By the time I lay exhausted on the bed, my eyes open to slits and my bones consisting of smooth jelly, Sato sat on the edge next to me staring at my bedroom door for the longest time. Then he leaned toward me and then ever so gently, he ran his rough fingertips along my chin. The gesture made my heart swell and strength surged into my limbs. If he wanted me to, I'd do anything to please him.

I looked forward to him doing this every night to me when we went to Nagasaki.

"May I comfort you?" I asked softly.

"You already have, *gekka bijin*," he replied, his voice hollow. "Sleep for now."

Gekka bijin. I was his queen of the night, his beauty under the moon. I'd do what I was told because that was what I always did.

Morning came and I woke up on my side. My mouth was dry and my body ached from lying in the same position for so long. Which could happen if I was tired enough. I rubbed an itchy spot on my forehead, then noticed something strange—I still had my wrist cuffs on. Sato always took them off me. The chains, which had secured me to the bed, hadn't been put away either.

"Sato?" I called out.

My apartment was deathly quiet. Even for nine in the morning. Limpish limbs and all, I managed to angle my legs out of the bed. Every muscle cried out in protest.

Since Sato had left before I had a chance to talk to him I decided to text him instead—only to find a post-it note on top of my cell:

I won't be coming back, Sophie. I'm sorry.

The note was written in barely legible English. That was it.

That was fucking it.

My hand barely cupped a piece of paper that felt like it weighed a ton.

So there'd been nothing to tell. Nothing that he couldn't say to my face. A cold shudder folded over me as I dropped the note onto the bed. Raw pain stabbed my stomach repeatedly and left me staring at the wall across the room. The bare wall that had all the photos I'd packed away.

How could I be such a fool? Such a fool to think that he'd whisk me away to Japan with him? I was a *gaijin*. A foreigner who spoke Japanese, but wasn't the Japanese girl his parents expected.

I curled into a ball and pulled the blankets over me, but nothing made the chill go away. The intensity rocked over me in waves. I cried. I even slept with my leather cuffs on. I didn't care anymore. His smell still lingered on the sheets and gave me little comfort.

Never again would I fall in love with a client.

A lesson learned since Sato had been my first.

Chapter Six

Sophie

Two years. That was how long I'd gone without any type of serious relationship. Let alone having sex. My lady parts were about to be declared a historical site at this point.

So when Mr. Quinn sent a text message this morning, I cringed a bit. After what went down last night, meeting him so early in the morning wasn't a wise idea, but a job was a job. He even sent his driver to pick me up and take me downtown to his studio apartment.

Two protein bars, he added via text. *Fresh coffee. Organic. One cream. Eight sugars.*

Just eight, huh? Talk about a one-way ticket to sugar shock.

Fetching the coffee and protein bars didn't take long, and soon enough, I was using the door code he gave me to enter his place. I anticipated a mess—the guy didn't have a personal maid anymore—but the place seemed vacant. Until I reached the kitchen.

Instead of using the desk in the living room, I found Xavier with papers scattered across the granite counter top. His laptop and cellphone was in front of him. He probably had a call on speakerphone. I took the hint and didn't speak.

"If we have to pay double for the resources, then do it," he said firmly.

He twisted to look at me. I extended his coffee to him and he took the drink with a nod. His hair was wet from a recent shower and he smelled delectable. Just as good as yesterday. My traitorous eyes lingered over his dark grey slacks and took in how perfectly they fit over his ass. He had the kind of shoulders a woman wanted to run her hands down. From the top down to the shoulder blades. The back of his neck, where his blond hair had been perfectly cut practically begged for me draw circles with my fingertips along the hairline. So sexy.

A sigh rested on my lips and I had to take a drink from the second coffee I bought for myself.

All business, right Sophie?

Then I got a good look at the laptop and saw a room full of people looking back at us.

Oh, shit. My face warmed and I had to stop my mouth from dropping open. He was in the middle of a friggin' video conference and I'd been *checking* him out this whole time. His ass, in particular. The whole west coast caught me looking him over like I wanted to strip him down and put on a show.

Beating a hasty retreat, I hurried to the living room.

A much better place to check out the view. Sunlight flittered through the floor to ceiling windows and I took in the view of downtown Boston. It was easy to get lost in my thoughts and think about the first time I looked at the Boston skyline. I've visited every single borough in NYC at least once, but Boston still had mystery, even after living here for a few years.

"Did you eat breakfast?" Xavier asked as he joined me at the window.

"I've already eaten," I quickly added. The most I'd done this morning was shower and throw on clothes while my roommates hibernated.

He chuckled. "I noticed you didn't eat the other protein bar, Miss Ashton."

"You asked for two bars so I assumed…"

"You assumed I wanted both," he finished.

Most clients didn't care if I ate. A businessman from Norway had me running ragged for ten hours straight handling conference arrangements for his employees. Just the thought of the final invoice I'd toss at the guy was what got me through the day.

This time I took the food Xavier gave me. I waited for him to interrupt my quick meal with questions, but all he did was sip his coffee and stare outside.

"You're not hungry?" I asked between bites.

"I ate earlier and worked out this morning. The place isn't too bad, by the way."

I nodded. "Glad you're settling in." Now that I was almost done, apprehension tried to sneak in, but I'd *tried* to prepare myself all night for this. For the moment where I'd be in front of him again and we'd begin this dance. With the last bite completed, I turned toward him. "Let's get down to business."

He offered a casual nod to show I had his full attention.

"The computer science department at MIT is hosting a luncheon and Nakamura will be present. Under normal circumstances, I'd advise attending the luncheon, but we need to stay under the radar at first. Our goal here isn't to be seen as stalkers—it's to gain *respect*. You have to be seen as a respected player on the field." Normally, when speaking with clients, I looked at them directly in the eyes, showing full engagement, but in the light of day, there was something arresting about the tiny grays flecks in his blue eyes. Focusing on his mouth was a no-no so I switched to his nose. Yeah, that wasn't the best spot either since every place on his face looked damn good.

"And how would I do that?" That was the golden question that made sleeping last night difficult for me. My job was to make it easier for my clients to be happy, relaxed, and enjoy their stay in Boston. No one had ever asked me to undertake such a mission.

I continued. "What I do advise is to attract the attention of his inner circle. In particular, Kaito Watanabe."

He crossed his arms. "The CEO of Watanabe Systems."

"Yep. I did my research last night and they attended Tokyo University together. Watanabe is a connoisseur of the arts. He has a foundation that is hosting an exclusive fundraiser the day after tomorrow."

"So a hefty check won't be enough?"

With a snap of his fingers I bet he could write a check for my yearly income without blinking. "That's not gonna cut it. That would get you into any of the foundation events, but in this close-knit community it's about respect and how others see you. Watanabe gets patrons, but only so many from outside the Japanese community. Making an appearance at the opera event they have this week will definitely get you on his radar. Only patrons are allowed and Watanabe personally greets every single patron."

"So it's settled then."

I nodded. Nice and easy. "Now, what we need—" I stopped to see where he was looking. The skin along my wrist, the place where he stared, was flush. He wasn't looking at my face as I'd expected. I sighed. Opening Pandora's box last night hadn't been a wise decision. I should've kept my private life and pain at home—it was for the best, but the cuffs were a comfort I refused to remove. They anchored me and I put them on like I always did. Almost as if they were a part of my wardrobe.

Morning light shone on Xavier's blond hair and the angelic halo around his head was nothing more than an illusion. A devilish heat danced in his eyes. It was as if he knew what I was wearing underneath my clothes and he could see through my thick chiffon top.

"What we need to talk about is what wasn't said between us last night," he said smoothly.

My eyebrow rose. "Am I missing something?"

I hadn't missed a damn thing.

He leaned forward and I froze. "The minute I returned to this apartment last night I haven't been able to stop thinking about you. I keep seeing you standing on that stairwell to my bedroom."

I tried to laugh, but the sound came out scratchy. "I already told you—"

"That you don't date your clients. And I already told you I'm not looking for a girlfriend. I don't need one."

"Even if I would be *vaguely* interested, we just met yesterday. I can't sleep with some guy I met the day before."

He smiled and my stomach fluttered from how damn beautiful he was. "You can find out anything you like about me. The press has taken pictures from every angle. A few I didn't like." He chuckled a bit.

His gaze swept over me from my hair, slid down to linger at my lips and then flittered over my collarbone like a lover's kiss. My throat dried further as his gaze flicked to my wrists. Heat filled my face. What was he thinking? It was almost as if I was rendered naked in this room, tied to the table, and he could see every vulnerable curve.

I finally managed to speak. "What we—you—should worry about right now, Mr. Quinn is the deal you want to secure."

"What if I want something more than the contract?"

I laughed. "I'm not sure what to tell you, but I don't think I'm the kind of girl you want anyway." I might not be the kind of girl for anyone. Getting left behind wasn't something I'd recovered well from. It was time to end this particular topic.

"You intrigue me, Miss Ashton."

"I bet you say that to *all* the girls at the office."

"No, I don't." His expression told me he was dead serious. Not even that brief upward quirk of his lips. Just his unwavering gaze. "I have very *particular* tastes."

I took a step back, but he didn't follow. "At the end of the day tomorrow, we need to attend to the fundraiser at the Boston Opera House. Once it's over we can—"

"We can see where things go from there." He wasn't joking.

I had a feeling this was coming after the dinner debacle and I was ready this time. "This is a high-end affair. Events at the opera house are red carpet parties with celebrities and dignitaries with deep pockets. I am your assistant, not your arm candy."

"I'd expect nothing more than that." While he nodded, I did the same, but on the inside I was stumbling over ideas as to how I'd pull this event off. The last client I had who secured front row tickets had her custom gown from Oscar de la Renta flown in from Paris. I didn't have that kind of income. *Yet.*

I said my goodbyes, but he didn't reply.

My phone buzzed in my pocket, but I ignored it. I

finally headed for the door and he joined me. Looks like escaping wasn't possible. His large hand warmed my back as we strode out of the apartment and to the elevator. By the time we reached outside, the plaza nearby was full of tourists. With the whole day ahead of us, I could handle a few matters with other clients, but the moment I reached for my phone to check my messages, his hand caught my forearm. I still wasn't used to the way he grabbed me. "Are you doing what I think you're doing?"

"I've reduced my load as much as possible to take care of you." From the corner of my eye, I noticed the nearby Bentley parked in valet. His driver hadn't made any move to pick me up.

I'd turned on the ringer so I could hear my phone ring this time.

"I almost forgot I needed to address that particular issue." His light blue eyes coursed through me and my breath caught. With his free hand he reached into his back pocket and pulled out an envelope. He placed it in my hand and waited.

"What's this?" I asked as I peeked inside.

The folded up piece of paper was a certified check. That many zeroes on a piece of paper should be illegal.

My undivided attention for the duration of his stay had been bought.

"Bigger check, right?" he asked softly.

I held in a groan. This was too much. "I need to say something before I agree to anything. Look, just like you, I'm running a business," I said. "I won't jeopardize every-thing I've built for one person."

"I told you yesterday what I expected. You've had time to prepare. Now you have the money to make it happen."

His demand was rather extreme and yesterday I thought I could find a way to slide around the requirement. Apparently, not. I held back a sigh. "Give me twenty-four hours and I'm all yours."

He nodded.

"Fine." At least I'd get a breather for a little bit to get my focus back in check. Having him so close to me was making it hard to concentrate.

He nodded and the Bentley came our way.

I got inside, but he had parting words for me before he shut the door. "Soon enough you'll belong to me, Miss Ashton."

Chapter Seven

Sophie

Lunchtime couldn't come soon enough after all the errands I ran today. Jesse kept texting me as I knocked out assignments like crazy.

"Are you sure you don't want me to do a few of these?" he asked me, his Alabama accent coming in thick through my cell.

"Oh, believe me, you'll have all the *fun* starting tomorrow." As a recent University of Alabama graduate, Jesse came to me looking for *any* job. Running errands, taking out the trash in my microscopic office in Cambridge. He'd moved here with his girlfriend less than a year ago, only to get dumped and left behind when she moved back to Nashville. Now he had a condo he had to pay for and only marketable skills in advertising. So I put his southern charm to work with my clients.

I have to tell you, the ladies in Back Bay and Beacon Hill *loved* a southern gentleman.

Naturally, in the middle of this mad dash to empty my

to-do list and dump the majority of it on my assistant, I had an important lunch to attend.

"Are you really going to use Skype during our lunch?" I asked Carlie over the phone as I weaved through a heavy crowd of diners at the Murder of Crows Diner. Restaurant row in the South End neighborhood was abuzz at this time of the day. Most of the folks I passed on Tremont Street were out and about to enjoy lunch.

Catching my friends wasn't hard, all I had to do was look for the tall Indian girl wildly gesturing and I'd find everyone. *Gotta love my roomie Penny.* Ever since we were kids in foster care in NYC, she always had a problem with volume control. She didn't give a damn who heard her either.

"The bitch is crazy, Griff." Penny's hand swung forward so fast, I waited for the drinks to go flying.

"Hey, everyone!" I slid into the free seat next to Griffin. Sitting next to Penny's flying hands wasn't wise.

"Good to hear Penny is present," Carlie added.

Griffin flashed me the look. The one he always gave me when he wanted someone to change the topic of conversation.

"Who's crazy, Penny?" After my long day, I had to know what golden advice she was bestowing upon Griff.

"It's the new lady he hooked up with," Penny began. "She's not kinky like us, but she's got something going on that smells like stalker." Other than friendship, I shared similar tastes to Carlie, Penny, and Griffin. While Penny and Griffin frequented the Boston BDSM club scene, Carlie and I didn't.

"Wait, what about the girl from last month?" I asked. "The one who called you talking about how she hadn't had sex in ten years and would hump the hardest thing she ran into?"

"I really need to stop letting you guys play matchmaker," Griff said with a snort. He tossed a chip into his mouth with a hard crunch. I didn't know why Griffin had such a hard time finding a serious relationship. Most women fell hard for his light brown eyes, short curly hair, and smooth brown skin. Like us, he grew up in the foster care system and didn't know his background.

Griff sighed. "We didn't even make it to the restaurant. She tried to unbutton my pants on the way."

"Way to go, Griff!" Carlie shouted from the phone. She sounded like she was munching on something. Maybe chips.

"If you weren't my best friend, Penny, I'd make you stop this madness." He appeared gruff about the matter, but he was never mad at her for long.

Carlie spoke with her mouth full. "Oh, c'mon! You couldn't hook her up for like *ten* minutes?"

"Ten?" he mouthed to me, apparently insulted.

Even I was bit insulted. He looked like at least a fifteen-minute man, but I'd never tell him to his face.

The waiter came by and took our orders.

Our food arrived and no one spoke while we ate—until the one person who didn't have a meal couldn't keep her mouth shut. "So everyone, did Sophie tell you she's moving to the UK to work with me?" Carlie said.

Penny's spoon stopped on the way to her mouth.

"I didn't say yes yet, Carlie," I said.

"Not yet, you haven't," Carlie replied with flourish.

"So you're leaving?" Penny asked.

"Not surprised," Griffin said softly. "First Mackenzie, now you."

I swallowed in a sigh. Our lunch crew had shrunk over the past year. "Mackenzie hates the snow."

"I get a free meal once a month. Is that gonna end

now?" Penny asked and I waited for the questions to begin. Not a single person paid for the food at this table thanks to me. Well, minus Carlie, but thanks to referring high-class clientele to Restaurant Row, we reaped the benefits with free food and drinks.

"If it's a great opportunity, you should take it," Griffin remarked, giving me his best smile.

Briefly, I leaned the side of my head against his wide shoulders. "Thanks, Griff, but I said I haven't taken the job yet." I caught Carlie's noise of disapproval. "I have a growing business here in Boston and right now might not be a good time to leave." There was no way in hell I was mentioning Xavier. Keeping him on track would take all my resources this month and preparing to relocate would keep me from doing my job.

As hard as I tried not to think about Xavier, he came to mind. Why did my insides quiver thinking about a man I'd just met yesterday?

"This is the next step up, Soph." My best friend's image wavered, but I caught her expression clearly. Her brown eyes flashed with an inner strength I wish I had and her cherry-red lips pursed into a confident grin. "I've already established my business here with exclusive clientele. This is the land of more than businessmen and media moguls. I've got *royalty*, m'dear. They've got money to burn and I've lined them up for you to pick them off the berry bushes."

Penny slid closer to the phone. "So how come you haven't offered me a job, Carlie?"

"I'd bore you, sweetheart." Carlie ran her hand through her blonde hair. Not that she needed too. Her hair was always perfect since her life was her work. She wasn't as social as Penny. Carlie and I knew what Penny wanted:

she wanted to settle down as someone's wife, but she also wanted someone who lived the BDSM lifestyle.

"That's true," Penny admitted. "I've got a really good thing going here. In a few months, I might find the right guy and be married."

A strange ache settled in my chest, but the feeling left as quickly as it had come. I would've done anything to hear a marriage proposal from Sato, even if our relationship hadn't been a conventional one. After one year seeing each other, we rarely spent a night apart—whether it was his place or mine. Except when he traveled to Japan. Back then every word he'd said seemed to have promises settled on the end of each phrase: *Someday I'd like for us to get a place together,* he had said back then. *I don't like you living alone. Someday I'd like to introduce you to my parents.*

But, he'd left me so that conversation had been a moot point, so marriage was an afterthought. Just like me.

Carlie kept going and it was hard to miss her remarks. "You coming here is a no-brainer. With your contacts in the northeastern US, we could shove aside the snotty bitches who think an American can't cut it among the Brits."

If I could close my ears, I would. This wasn't the time to contemplate the benefits. A new place might do me some good though.

A new land and a new start.

Maybe by the time I started working with Carlie, I'd forget about my new client for good.

But just one errant thought of Xavier—his brooding gaze, his imposing presence—left me wondering if forgetting was even possible.

Chapter Eight

Sophie

A perfect morning could be made with the perfect egg dish.

With the weight of Carlie's offer on my mind, I settled into my Sunday morning routine. First and foremost, I worked on accomplishing the most important task of the day: Crafting the perfect Eggs Benedict. And I'm not talking about just flipping some eggs on an English muffin and calling it a day. For me, life was about accomplishing goals. Two years ago, I had a goal to achieve near fluency in Japanese. On any given Sunday, a few years ago, you'd find me perched on the end of my bed going over Japanese verbs with flourish.

I go. I went.

Ikimasu. Ittekimashita.

Over and over again until I babbled Japanese in my sleep and I could communicate with Sato in his mother tongue. I was fluent now, but speaking Japanese was just a reminder of all the work I put into a man who casually pushed my love aside.

Today, my aspirations were a bit simpler: conquer all the recipes in a worn old cookbook from the library called *Excellent Eggs and You*. I have to say it's a pretty deep, thought-provoking book from cover to cover.

Every step in the recipe, from preparing the sauce that went over the eggs, to the garnish added on top, set my mind at ease as I worked barefoot in the quiet kitchen. This dish was just another tidbit of knowledge to share with my clients. Another conversational piece in my arsenal. 'Cause who didn't like to talk about food?

By the time I placed the exquisite sauce on my egg, my cell phone bleeped with a new message. I ignored it and admired my masterpiece. Until the phone beeped again so I snatched my cell off the counter to peek.

You owe me, the text from my old friend Franklin read.

About time he came through for me. When I moved here from New York, one of the first people I connected with in Boston was Franklin. At sixty-five, he was one of the oldest vintage gown seamstresses in the area. With the right budget, he could cram you into the best designer dresses your money could buy. Clothes made the woman, and for someone in my industry, I had to fit in.

Don't bother eating for the rest of the day, Sophie, he added.

I sighed. I had a great deal of money right now, but finding the right gown at the last minute put me in a bind. For a brief moment, I considered making up an ailing distant cousin who was recovering from cat lady syndrome, but he needed me.

He wouldn't accept the excuse either way. *I don't take no for an answer unless there is a valid excuse*, he'd said when we'd met.

Other than avoiding him due to this attraction I couldn't shake, I had no other excuse.

My phone rang and Penny's picture, along with the name *Penny Rules the World* showed up on the screen. That name was her doing—not mine. I let the phone ring again before I took the call. "Hey, Penny."

"Did you miss my last message, Soph?" Penny sounded breathless, too. Her voice sounded far away for a second. "I sort of need a favor."

I had yet to get any message from her this morning.

"Most favors aren't of the *sort of* type."

"I found someone *perfect* for Griffin."

Again? "Sounds great."

"Anyway, one of my friends in Back Bay has a close friend who is here on business from St. Louis. He's into kink and she says he's a sweetheart. We're meeting this afternoon to chat, but I kind of made the mistake of arranging the brunch during my job."

Her job, as in, her as an *at-home phone-sex operator* job.

"Oh." I rummaged through the cupboards and found two month-old protein bars. *You're a cruel man, Franklin.* The Eggs Benedict smelled so damn good.

"All you have to do is step in like the last time you did this for me," Penny said simply. Taking over this kind of thing wasn't simple.

"I don't know. I have a lot to do." Like hope and pray I won't have to be sewn into my dress.

"The last time you were in a bind I was the Indian girl who stepped in to help you with that Hindi event." With expert precision she tossed the race card into the conversation. She was my go to girl for such questions.

"What time?" If I said yes I could wrap up this conversation quickly.

"I'll send you an email with the particulars. Show up in

my private chat room at four and be ready with your toys. He likes to be tied up and spanked for all the naughty things he did during the week."

We finally ended the conversation and I wondered what the hell I'd gotten myself into. With a sigh, I rotated the plate and admired my handiwork.

The food—which now I couldn't eat—seemed perfect. My mood not so much.

NOT LONG BEFORE four p.m., I prepped for Penny's phone call. I'd already made the trip to Franklin's boutique and now I had one beautiful black dress. Nothing as fancy as what many of my clients would wear, but it was floor-length, strapless, and if anyone asked, I could say the dress was made by Alexander McQueen. That name alone implied haute couture. No one needed to know the gown was from a collection from over five years ago.

Now that my dress was set, I had to look the part. While I added large curlers into my hair, I prepped for the call, placing my supplies on my desk. The short hand on the clock was quickly approaching two. I surveyed my equipment: A riding whip, a thick belt, and a chain about the length of my wrist. The equipment of a budding Foley artist.

On the appointed time, I picked up the phone and made the call. I didn't have to wait long for Penny's client to click in.

"Hey, stranger," I said, trying to sound like I was cheerful and not someone who was filling in for a friend.

"Is that you, Penny?" a man with a thick Southern accent asked. Even Jesse wasn't that hard to make out.

"Your pretty little Penny is getting…polished at the

bank so I'm here to take care of you." I introduced myself as Shelley and I learned his name was Bill.

"Your voice is making me hard already, sweetheart." His voice was kind of sexy in a way. Deep and thick. "I've been so bad this week."

Time to pull out the toys to play. The sooner Bill got off, the sooner I could finish getting ready for the opera at 6. Xavier was picking me up at 5:15.

I grabbed a belt and flicked it to produce a hard *thwack*. "A naughty cowboy like you should get tied up nice and proper."

In exquisite detail, I described over the phone how I'd blindfold him first. "I'm going to run a silk scarf across those shoulders of yours, then over your hard nipples."

Getting blindfolded by Sato was one of the many pleasurable experiences I'd enjoyed. As a sub, I loved a partner who loved to be in control. My anticipation built faster. My orgasms became earth shattering. Every minute he delayed the inevitable turned me on even more. Since I didn't know what was coming every inch of my body tingled, wishing he'd touch me. My patience was legendary for the reward he offered. Just thinking about those pending orgasms made my toes curl.

Bill groaned. Time to get back to work.

"Yes, please…" Bill gasped.

"Close those eyes."

"Mmm. I like that, baby." He moaned, most likely clenching the flesh of his erection while he listened to me.

Now that Bill's eyes were closed—I wasn't sure about that in reality—but now I could move onto the fun part. Next came the chains and sounds of ropes getting yanked and tied. Time to tie up my cowboy to the post for play time.

"What naughty things have you done this week, Bill?" I slapped my rider's whip on the table. A nice sharp sound.

I hoped and prayed Lana was still studying. She'd had her headphones on and she was doing an air guitar move over her mountain of books when I'd grabbed a bottle of water.

"I can't stop jacking off when I get home from work. The lady at the department store is getting suspicious about all the lady lotions I'm buying."

Umm, okay…

Flick! I slapped the table again. "You like it when I make those ass cheeks pink, don't you, Bill?" I purred.

"Yes, Ma'am…"

While I was telling Bill about how long and hard I'd spank him, I got an email from a sous chef regarding the approval for the catering of an old west theme barbecue. *Ha! Go figure!*

With a pleasurable sigh, Bill finished stroking his little cowpoke to completion—right as my bedroom door opened.

Chapter Nine

Sophie

Lana stared at me, her mouth agape.

I now had a guest and I was standing next to my desk with a riding whip in one hand and a belt in the other. Massive green curlers must've added quite the maniacal effect. One thing was for certain, after getting caught today by Lana, this would be the last time I did any *personal* favors for Penny.

"I called your name, but you didn't answer," Lana blurted. "There's some guy named Chris at the door. He said Mr. Quinn was waiting for you outside. Who's he?"

Oh shit. Why was he here so early? At least he wasn't the one who opened the door.

Lana looked me over with an amused grin. "You sure take customer service to the next level."

I turned away from her and quickly wrapped up the call with Bill. He'd already crossed the finish line, so there wasn't much to discuss.

"Don't we have a policy about knocking?" I asked

while I scrambled to pull my curlers out. She was halfway into my room before I could say more.

"You were making so much noise—" Lana began. "Can I *borrow* that?" She reached for the riding whip, a mischievous gleam to her dark blue eyes.

I groaned. "How long has Mr. Quinn been waiting?"

"Not too long."

I opened the garment bag with my Alexander McQueen dress and placed it over my chest. The sweetheart bodice had been hand-stitched and silk chiffon fabric was delicate and soft along my fingertips. "All the favors I owe Franklin will be worth it. I miss dressing up."

Lana tapped the end of the riding whip into her palm as I put on my gown.

"Why don't you borrow it before I give it back to him?" I asked. If a hot dress would get that poor girl out of a studying stupor, I was game.

Now that my dress was on there wasn't much left to do. I discarded my leather cuffs and left them in my bedside drawer. This sleeveless gown wouldn't hide my secrets. My fingers flew through my dark hair, teasing out the curls until they hung in loose waves to my shoulders. I already had my garters on and my stilettos were waiting for me by the door. Time to impress Mr. Quinn with my networking ninja prowess.

"And go where?" She gave a dry laugh. "A dress like that needs man candy and right now I'm supposed to be on a dick diet."

I rolled my eyes. Books wouldn't relieve her stress. I knew that for sure.

With a final check in the mirror, I was ready to go. Not bad for a mad scramble. "And Lana," I called her as she left the room with my crop in hand, "punishment comes first, then reward."

She snorted. "Now I need to find someone to punish."

By the time I got into the Bentley, I was a bit winded. The sun had yet to set and I felt a bit awkward leaving my place in something so formal. Once I got settled into the seat though, everything slid into place. I was Sophie Ashton wearing a couture gown on the way to the opera. Just another day on the job.

"You're early," I remarked, keeping my gaze straight away. He looked so good it hurt my eyes. His shortly cropped hair had been styled to perfection and his finely tailored clothes and dignified air made me believe for a moment that he was my date.

"I wanted us to go over any last minute details over drinks." His deep voice was honey to my ears. I couldn't miss the way he glanced over me with appreciation. Before I could open my mouth, he added, "You keep skipping meals so I wanted to make sure you were taken care of, Miss Ashton."

A protest right now seemed appropriate, but we were already dressed and ready for the opera. The space I kept between us though didn't seem like it was enough. To keep myself occupied, and my mind on business, I went over scenarios with Xavier on how to interact with Watanabe to the best people for him to impress. My mouth kept moving, but Xavier's heated gaze made it hard for me to focus.

By the time we were on our way downtown to the opera house, my skin hummed again and I couldn't sit still in the seat. Again and again I reminded myself he'd be gone in a few weeks. This hunger that made my breath catch and my body tremble would go away. This was nothing more than an attraction I had to get past.

That became easier said than done when he finally spoke. "You look breathtaking right now. You'll be a great asset tonight. I know people, but there are many social circles here in Boston and you know them better than me."

So all the time I spent securing a proper dress had been for the benefit of attracting attention and not because he liked how I looked. I shoved that thought aside and focused on the obvious: at least he knew my strengths very well.

"All we're doing is the benefit and then I need to go home," I said.

"Naturally." His grin said otherwise.

Breathtaking, he'd said. I tried not to let myself react to such words. I'd done everything I could to make sure I looked my best. I touched the curls going down my back to make sure they were in place.

"I've been wanting to do that all evening." His fingers twitched.

"*Do* my hair?" My lips pursed. "Now this is a new talent I didn't know about."

He reached for me and stopped midway. A part of me screamed for me to lean toward him. *Don't give him a foot because he'll take a yard.* And yet, I wanted him to reach out and touch a tendril. I wanted him to take a fistful and pull my head back. If he asked me comply, would I do it?

"Have you ever seen the painting called the *Water Serpent*?" he asked casually.

I shook my head. "The name sounds familiar though."

"It's an erotic painting by Gustav Klimt with a woman holding a man. Klimt had a thing for the naked female form. He found symbolism in what others would find overtly sexual."

I chuckled. "I've yet to do any naked posing for art."

"No, I'm sure you haven't, but you remind me of the woman in that painting. The milky complexion to your skin. The way your hair falls down your back."

My breath caught and I had to turn away from him to take in the lights of downtown Boston.

Thank goodness we pulled up to the opera house before I got a chance to lose it. He was almost close enough to see all my secrets and none of them I wanted to tell.

Chris opened the door for us. Xavier emerged first and I followed him. The sounds of busy streets erupted around us, but all I could focus on was him and the fact he stood so close to me. Flashing lights from photographer's cameras flashed around us, pulling me out of the moment.

You're not on a date, Sophie.

I reminded myself I was his assistant for the evening and any inquiries to his company would reflect such.

"This way, Mr. Quinn," one man with a camera called.

Xavier paused, turning so that his hand hovered over my back. So tantalizingly close, yet not close enough to touch me. Ever since I'd met him on the plane, he'd avoided touching me for some reason. I briefly glanced at the flashing lights, but my stomach was churning on the inside. The last thing I needed was a headline in the Boston Globe: *"Concierge Phenom passes out in the bright lights and flashes her Wal-Mart panties to the world."*

"You all right?" he whispered in my ear.

"Of course." I gave him the smile I gave everyone.

Amusement shined in his blue eyes. "Of course."

It was hard not to get caught up in the excitement. A long row of limousines waited to bring more patrons for the event tonight. The people who got out were dressed in dazzling evening wear from Valentino to Herve Leger. Wealth had a smell from the heady citrus cologne the men wore to the delicate, expensive floral perfumes the ladies dabbled behind their necks.

"Do you always smile like that when you lie?" Xavier

had more to say as we entered the building. Heat filled my face. I kept my mouth shut and continued to walk beside him, all the while taking in the signs for upcoming events. *The Nutcracker. Sleeping Beauty*. Tonight's piece was *Pelléas et Mélisande*.

I couldn't believe he outright said that, but this was Xavier Quinn I was talking about here.

A beautiful grand chandelier shined above our heads. I'd been in this building many times before, but I was always delighted each time. Acquaintances who grew up in the area told me the opera house had been renovated over a decade ago and now the original glory had returned. I could see it in the fine marble on the floor to the gold leaf finishes on the walls. The carpets and tapestries added an old world flair that made this experience even more fairy-tale-like.

"I take that as a yes," he added when I remained quiet.

"No comment, Mr. Quinn."

We joined the crowd enjoying refreshments in the lobby. The stairs to the theater lay ahead. Now that we were in the thick of things, I couldn't miss how others glanced in our direction. Women whispered inquiries to their friends. Men remarked on the new player on the field. And I was standing next to him.

Using my trained eye, I scanned over the crowd and I noted familiar faces. Even prior and current clients.

"Champagne?" Xavier placed one in my hand.

"Thanks."

The drink went down smooth. I turned to look at him from the corner of my eye. "You ready to do this?"

"Do your thing." He extended his hand toward the crowd.

As we weaved through the crowd, Xavier became chatty. "How many people here do you know?"

"Too many to count," I said with a laugh.

I introduced him to a few businessmen first. Going all out eager with the men associated with Nakamura wasn't wise. Step one was to build buzz.

During the whole time, I tried to focus while Xavier stood close enough for our bodies to almost touch. For the bare skin of my shoulder to brush against his. To anyone who looked at us, they'd most likely see us guiding me through the crowd having a good time, but to me tonight felt like punishment. A torture of sorts that made it harder for me to focus.

"Will Nakamura be here tonight?" he asked, looking over at Watanabe as he greeted one of his guests.

"Definitely." The timing had to be perfect for his introduction to Watanabe. "He's one of Watanabe's patrons, but I don't want you to approach him yet."

"And why is that?" He was close to me again, his minty breath warming the side of my face. A master of seduction that rivaled Sato's attentions. The tension in my stomach grew uncomfortable.

"There's a good reason why I always do what I do," I managed. "Just like you told me."

"And you wouldn't have me do something unless you have a good reason."

"Precisely."

I still held my empty champagne glass. Any intentions to put the glass down vanished. Any distraction was welcome so I settled on conversation.

"I love the tapestries in here," I remarked. On the other side of the room, I caught sight of Nakamura coming in with his wife.

"See something you like?" Xavier asked.

"Many of these are on loan from overseas." I pointed the nearest one that put me in the line of sight for Nakamura's approach to Watanabe. "That one I believe is from an exhibit in Scotland. The first time I saw it was in Paris."

"So you've travelled internationally?"

Did he think I was some rookie concierge who wasn't familiar the places I took my clients? "Of course. I might've even seen more places than you have. I've been almost everywhere—except Japan and Malaysia. Three times last year to South America and I might be the only person to say I've seen most of the hidden gems in the London airport during my countless layovers."

He gave a small smile. "I've never had the opportunity to travel for pleasure."

Now that surprised me. Around us, the crowd shifted. We had less than five minutes to go before the show began. My gaze shifted toward Watanabe and he followed my lead. A small line formed to greet him.

"Wouldn't you at least go to Cancun or Monaco or some place like that for yachting?" I asked.

"Sounds like fun, but in the business I'm in, I travel to make more money for my company."

He chuckled when I made us walk more quickly so that we could get in line to the theatre right in front of Nakamura. "All work and no play..." I began.

"Makes Jack a very rich man," he finished.

"Makes Jack a tired man," is what I wanted to say.

"You had to have gone on vacation once." Nakamura was right behind us, but I didn't want him to go silent. I wanted to see the real Xavier at this moment.

"Not once, Miss Ashton. Wait, I went to Disney Land with my family. Does that count?"

"Kind of." Not really. I'd always imagined a man like Xavier Quinn lounging and eating olives on a yacht off Hawaii. Bikini clad women offering him drinks and saucy conversation. I'd yet to do anything like that.

Xavier laughed.

"What?"

"I remember the day when my brother Marcus broke his leg at the park. At the time I thought he'd ruined the whole trip, but now that I look back at least we were all together at the time."

I wanted to ask further what he meant by that, but we finally reached Kaito Watanabe.

The older businessman looked to be no more than fifty, but I knew he was in his late sixties. He smiled, extending his hand toward Xavier. "I'm pleased to see you came, Mr. Quinn. I was pleasantly surprised to hear of your kind donation."

Xavier didn't grasp Watanabe's hand with both of his in the manner that the Japanese prefer, but Xavier was an American so that faux pas could be ignored. "The pleasure is mine. I'm always looking for new organizations to support through the Quinn Foundation. The work you do here for traditional arts is astounding."

Watanabe briefly looked at me. I bowed and greeted him in Japanese. After that I remarked, in Japanese, how excited Xavier was to give to such an important cause and how Xavier wanted to be involved in future partnerships with a man as esteemed and experienced as him. Xavier's company made a lot more money than Watanabe's, but that didn't matter right now. Respect did.

Poor Xavier had no idea what I was saying, but he kept smiling—like I wanted him to do.

Right behind us, Nakamura waited, but he heard every word.

Watanabe nodded. Then he turned to his assistant who extended a card. *Bingo!* I took it with both hands and a bowed head.

"Mr. Nakamura." Xavier nodded his way.

I cringed on the inside, my plan crumbling for an offhand introduction after Nakamura heard us talking to Watanabe.

Nakamura simply nodded and Watanabe turned to him. Our opportunity vanished to have Watanabe introduce Xavier to him in an offhand manner. Damn.

Now we had no choice but to say our thanks and head up the stairs to theatre.

I sighed. Being disappointed would get in the way of coming up with a new plan. I had the whole evening to figure something out.

We went up a well-lit stairwell to Xavier's private booth. I focused on going up each step, but instead my mind wandered and I kept thinking about the man behind me. Could he see the way the dress fit my curves or the way my hips began to sway as if they had a mind of their own?

By the time we reached the booth and slipped into the red velvet seats, my whole body hummed. Ignoring the feeling was futile, even with my face forward and my gaze set on the stage. There were plenty of sights to drink in from the ornate painted ceiling with intricate cherub carvings to the beautiful crystal chandeliers hung along the walls.

The massive room dimmed and murmurs from the crowd floated up to us. The performance would begin soon and give me the distraction I wanted.

A waiter arrived with more champagne, but I didn't look over my shoulder. Finally, Xavier spoke to me.

"Would you like some champagne?" he whispered. His breath was warm on my neck. I didn't dare turn toward him. My imagination churned out vivid images I couldn't push away: His lips trailing across my neck. His hand pressed against thigh.

Xavier handed me the glass and I gratefully downed the drink to sate my parched throat.

His left arm was close enough to warm my right side and all I could do to keep myself in check was keep my hands in my lap. Even intertwining my fingers didn't settle my senses.

The orchestra's music began, the horns softly playing as the first act of *Pelléas et Mélisande* started.

"Have you seen this piece before?" he asked.

His words broke through to me. I dared a quick peek and his dark, mesmerizing stare forced my lips to part. My throat to dry.

"Yes. A year ago," I managed.

"Damn it, Miss Ashton," he breathed. The side of his mouth turned slightly with a devilishly grin. "You need to stop looking at me like that."

"Like what?" My gaze flicked to the man and woman singing on the stage. Her melodic voice further softened my already molten insides.

"Like you're begging me to touch you."

Was it that obvious? He had yet to touch me again and I was close to begging. Even with the guilt of what I wanted nipping at me. Were my eyes betraying what my body felt? My body for damn sure didn't care that he was a client and not a man who had similar interests to mine.

Instead of waiting for a response from me, his left hand drifted to rest on his knee. His fingers flexed, the movement wonderfully hypnotic.

Would one touch ruin everything?

We sat like that for some time, sipping the champagne through the first two acts. Then the third act began with Mélisande sitting at a tower window singing as she combed her long hair. Pelléas looked at her longingly and I wanted to look away. As hard as I tried to ignore

Xavier, his hand still rested on his knee, ever so close to mine.

His head drifted toward me, yet he didn't touch me. "It's amazing how Debussy showed how much Pelléas longed for Mélisande. Even though she could never be his."

My heart sped up and the truth hit me hard.

She could never be his.

He continued. "As a woman married to his brother, she haunted him in a way, her very presence bringing out a side of him he thought he could contain." Finally, he brushed the back of his hand against my knee. I sucked in a breath. Next came a firm squeeze along my mid-thigh. *Pure. Bliss.* Just one touch had me trembling. "Passion. Longing."

I tried to watch the play, but my gaze kept drifting to my clenched hands in my lap. The large hand on my thigh. Waiting was something I did so well, so why was my resolve crumbling so quickly?

Then his hand wandered up my thigh, dipping briefly near my sex, until he gripped my left wrist. The need to respond to him was intense. But the very idea of giving in made me freeze. Only once did I dare to look at him—he continued to watch the show intently—while my breath quickened. His thumb circled my palm. Sparks danced along my skin from slow, yet deliberate touch.

I closed my eyes and told myself to tell him to let go of my hand.

Don't do this again, Soph.

But there was no escaping him and I let it happen. He was closer now, his breath warming my cheek. "I'm going to kiss you, Sophie," he declared firmly.

But instead of kissing my lips, he drew me onto his lap. The fullness of my dress didn't deter him. The music continued to play. He kissed the point where my wrist began. Right above my pulse point. Like a leopard sampling his prey, he ran his lips, then his tongue over the most sensitive parts of the skin along my hand.

All the while, he whispered to me, his voice thick. "I control myself in all things, Miss Ashton." The grip along my wrist tightened until I hissed. *So good. Damn him.*

"But your beautiful eyes make me want to do things to you that I shouldn't..." Watching him do this to me was one of the hottest things I'd ever seen in my life. "Things that I told myself I wouldn't do with an employee."

I was breathless by the time he looked at me again. Our lips were mere inches apart. I could practically taste the alcohol he'd sampled. Settled in his lap with my head tilted toward his, our bodies were too close to prevent the inevitable from happening. He captured my lips and I unclenched my fists. My reservations floated away along with the tension in my limbs.

In contrast to Melisande softly singing, every part of Xavier was hard. His body unyielding, his lips firm and hungry against mine. His tongue darted into my mouth and I moaned. I sagged against him, opening my lips further to invite more. Our tongues danced, dueling until he pulled back with a violent tremble.

He was as breathless as I was. The subtle upward thrust of his hips made my thighs clench with need. "There are so many things I could do to you..." He drew in a deep breath.

"Like what?" I tried to rise from his lap, but his arms locked around me.

My protest waited on my lips, but I couldn't bring myself to speak. While the final act played, he couldn't see a thing. His lips rested against my cheek. Long enough for me to memorize the shape of his lips. For the stubble along his chin to tickle me.

Again and again I told myself to get up, that I was letting myself fall into a game that would leave me wounded. But Sato had never treated me like this. Not in public, anyway. Sato's passions played out in private, away from the prying eyes of others.

By the time the final fifth act ended, I resigned myself to getting up. As easy as that idea came, once the lights turned back on, the stark reality of what had happened made it hard for me to look at him. This was my employer and I was sitting in his lap. The assistant who let her boss kiss her hand like a lover.

I tried to stand and he let me do so.

"Did you enjoy the piece?" I held in a sigh. What else could I say? *Let's go out for drinks.* Or even what plans do you really have for me other than seduction? But I knew my place and after hearing him say he didn't want a relation-ship, at the rate I was going I'd end up in bed. When it was time for him to leave I'd be alone again.

"The performers are very talented. Your company made the piece all the more pleasurable. Of course."

"Of course." What else could I say? I clasped my hands together to keep myself in check. His dark gaze never wavered.

"We should join the others for refreshments."

He slowly stood and I couldn't keep myself from taking in his long, lean legs. The need to look between his legs to see what had pressed against me flicked at my mind, but I kept my gaze where it needed to be.

The loud crowd was welcomed once we descended the stairs from the theatre, but I couldn't go far without following him. His scent was all over me and I couldn't stop thinking about his lips. Every time he spoke to someone my gaze drifted to them. Every time he shook someone's hand I imagined his hand touching me.

By the time we reached the lobby, I managed to bring Sophie back into play. This was where I thrived. Meeting new people and making new connections. I was talking with a bank vice president of a major bank in the north-east, when Xavier leaned toward my ear.

"I see an associate of mine, I'll be back in a bit." I quickly nodded, welcoming a bit of space between us. It would be far too easy for me to want to follow him, to continue to feel his hand on my back, but this was for the best.

After chatting with the manager about how I could help his wife plan a golfing trip for her and her friends, I continued to stroll around and introduce myself to new people.

But then I stopped cold to see a familiar back. The shape was all too familiar and feminine. She was short and shapely with the most beautiful black hair. I'd seen her a few times two years ago and she always wore the same designer perfume.

My heart skittered.

Don't look, Sophie. Maybe if you don't look, she won't really be there.

I prayed Komiko Haruto didn't turn around.

But it was too late. The two women accompanying her saw me and whispered in my direction.

Komiko turned around and a kind smile touched her lips. For a woman who had to be no more than fifty, she had a girlish grace and a mischievous glint to her dark brown eyes that made her look no older than thirty-five.

"*Sophie-san*, is that you, dear?" she called to me in Japanese.

My insides turned to ice. What was she doing here?

Was the rest of Sato's immediate family in town? He couldn't be here. In the two years since he'd left me behind, he had yet to set foot on American soil.

Back when I dated Sato, I only met his relatives twice during family gatherings. The Harutos had lavish affairs, but I always felt like an outsider—which is one of the many reasons why I learned Japanese. It was all too often I felt like there was a barrier between Sato and me. He spoke English fluently, but his family didn't. Learning his mother tongue seemed like the best way to scale the divide between his world and mine.

Oh, what a fool I was back then.

Once I'd learned Japanese, I was invited to spend time with Komiko and she took me under her wing, so to speak. Having someone to practice with had been appreciated, but once Sato left me, for some reason my association with Komiko vanished, too.

Resolve left me and circled the room before I moved. With a curt bow, I greeted her and the other ladies. "It's a pleasure to see you, Komiko-san," I began. If there was hesitation to my voice, she didn't react.

"One of my nieces, I'm sure you remember Aoki, is getting married this week." Komiko was all smiles. "The lucky couple wanted to celebrate with their fellow classmates at Harvard."

I nodded in agreement. "Sounds wonderful. You'll have to send me her contact information so I may congratulate her properly."

One of Komiko's friends chuckled. "Why would you send a gift?"

Somehow I kept my hands from forming fists. There wasn't a reason other than being nice to a former acquaintance. I had no ties to the Haruto family any longer.

"Of course, she'd send a gift," Komiko said. "*Sophie-san*

is a *friend* of the family." The others nodded as if Sato's aunt had given her final word and discussion wasn't necessary.

Embarrassment warmed my cheeks. Based on past experiences, I surmised that Komiko meant no ill will. She stated the facts and that made the ache I'd suppressed for so long flare like unhealed wound.

I glanced up to see Xavier had joined us. Out of all the times for him to return, why did it have to be now?

"Is this your date?" Komiko asked. The two other women eyed him with appreciation.

"This is a business associate of mine." I made formal introductions between everyone. Xavier bowed properly, mimicking my movements from earlier. He even tried to return the greeting in Japanese. He stumbled a bit, but he wasn't short on confidence.

Now that everyone knew each other, Komiko's friends said their goodbyes and drifted away, engrossed in their own conversation about what they planned to do once they returned to Japan. Komiko turned to face me. A flicker of pity crossed her face. "I won't be in town long, but we should have tea if our paths should cross again."

"I'd like that," I said, knowing very well the tea would never happen.

We parted ways and soon I was alone with Xavier. Silence lingered between us, but willing my mouth to move was impossible. Shame pressed me to the floor.

"Are you ready to leave?" he finally asked me.

Could he read the tension in my shoulders? The doubt circling my stomach?

"For drinks, perhaps?" he added.

I nodded. "Yes, to leave, but I'd like a rain check on those drinks."

"Another time then."

When he pressed his hand against my back I flinched, so he withdrew. My mood had soured considerably and meeting Komiko was a sound reminder I shouldn't place myself in a position to fall for a man again who truly didn't want me.

Chapter Ten

Xavier

The gym equipment beckoned me in the morning. No matter how sore I was from the day before, or maybe how much I hadn't slept from coding all night, I still got up like clockwork at 5:30 a.m. to work out. Old habits from high school and college died hard.

I found fresh water bottles and organic green tea in the fridge and chuckled. Miss Ashton said she'd take care of me. For the past two days I couldn't stop thinking about our evening at the opera. I'd even tried to call her last night... That night at the theatre, my steadfast resolve had crumbled away. Every nerve ending in my body sparking like crazy until I couldn't suppress the need to possess her. I'd only meant to reach for her once. A brief brush against her leg. But every time she looked at me, I fell into the depths of those pretty blues. That night I wanted to give into temptation.

I made my way from my studio to the gym, a bit concerned at my lack of self-control. At least I could knock out an hour or two and work my frustrations out on the equipment—even if I did feel a bit stiff today. My back was good, but my right leg protested on the way. No matter the pain, routine was routine.

Out of nowhere, I thought of Rosalie's laugh when I got out of bed early.

"I think you might love your gym more than me," she used to say. She always said that before she left for work. Her job was her first love, while I happened to be the man who satisfied her desire to submit on the weekends. I was a fool even back then, giving into her every desire. In return, I assumed she'd fall in love with me if we spent more time together. A painful lurch in my chest I hadn't felt in a long time twitched. Little did I know time was something we didn't have in abundance. Memories flashed through my mind of hospitals to specialists folded over me and I pushed them back where they belonged—in the past. After Rosalie's giant cell myocarditis diagnosis, everything changed in a way I never saw coming. I went from a casual sexual relationship, where I thought I was falling in love, to being a support system for a woman with a fatal autoimmune disorder. After being with Rosalie, maybe I hadn't learned my lesson.

Once inside the gym, I nodded to the other few guys who came in early. Fellow fitness enthusiasts.

"Morning, Xavier." The sole guy at the treadmill threw a nod my way. Every time I came, Bob the Headhunter, as I called him, worked out on the treadmill next to mine when I did my run.

He didn't break a beat in his stride, casually sprinting for about an hour before he got off to get ready and head to work.

"Looking good, man," he always said that first. "How's the hunt going?"

"So far so good."

"Like I told you, if you need an executive level job, I'm your man. Been finding gigs for folks like yourself for years now." He looked me over as if he could see every secret or flaw I had. When I first got here I thought he recognized me. "I bet I could get you a job with a firm in Philly in a day or two. You like insurance?"

Apparently, he didn't know the face of the guy who constructed the electronics on his phone.

"I'm good, thanks." I smiled like I always did and refused any offers. By the time I finished running, I went through my work out routine.

Once I got in the zone, it was easy to forget about my troubles. Every time I completed a set of weights, I tried to focus on the present, but the past seemed to creep back in. I began a set of pulls, then muscle memory kicked in and I fell into an old habit of seeing myself and filling my thoughts with an unyielding drive. During each pull I saw myself growing stronger as the exercise tore apart muscles and built them back up.

Back in high school and college, every workout was an endeavor toward a greater goal of becoming a better athlete. That meant no sleeping in as I left my house while my parents slumbered. Most of the time, the only other person who was awake at the same time was Marcus.

When I went to workout, he worked a part-time job at one of our family resorts as soon as he was old enough to drive. At an early age, Marcus gave as much effort into his work ethic as I did at sports. Time and time again, I heard Dad talk—when he thought we weren't listening—about how Marcus didn't have a lick of talent.

"The boy can't figure his way out of a paper bag, but at least he knows a hard day's labor," Dad used to say when we were in high school.

Shit like that always bothered me because I looked up to Marcus. As my older brother, he was the one who kicked my ass when shit went down and I didn't give a damn.

To this day I still wonder if Marcus was happy being the family savior after I fell from grace.

In the middle of the set, a loud noise jarred my attention and I paused. The burn in my arms felt good and memories of long sessions came to mind, but that wasn't me anymore.

My phone buzzed in my pocket. I'd been at it for longer than usual. It was practically seven and any overseas VPs for Silver Sparrow Systems hadn't poked me yet.

The message was from Sophie: *Great news. Be ready this afternoon for a golf outing. Got an invite from Watanabe.*

So golf today, eh?

"Do you know how to play?" I typed in reply.

"Kind of…"

Now that made me chuckle. I rested my sweaty forehead on the wall below the bar and found it hard not to imagine her lying in bed at such an early time in the morning. The delicious thought made my cock jerk with approval, but I squashed the thought. That wasn't the Sophie I'd come to know. She'd most likely be dressed in a suit, her hair already in place.

At least she wasn't mad at me or anything. We'd parted poorly. After she spoke to those three Japanese women, the spark in her seemed to fade. Her bright smile faltered and she clasped her hands as if intimidated. I'd wanted to spend more time with her afterwards, but the idea didn't seem appropriate at the time.

So I waited patiently and now Sophie had placed another opportunity my way to meet Nakamura.

Another message: *We'll meet at The Country Club at 9:30 am sharp.*

Nine seemed rather early. Perhaps I'm supposed to meet them at ten and she didn't want me to be late. *Very clever, Ms. Ashton*, I thought.

Another text message came in. *I've already made arrangements to have a set of your preferred clubs available and a caddy.*

She made no mention of her participation, but there was one thing I was certain of: Soon enough I'd be able to see her again and I had a question about a little message I left on her phone last night.

～

Sophie

The clouds appeared to threaten our plans with rain, but once I met Xavier in front of the main house on the golf course, the skies cleared. An opportunity like this was perfect. Nakamura would be golfing with us.

So I arrived early with a game plan and waited for him in front of the vast, three-story clubhouse painted in bright yellow. History permeated from everything and I could almost imagine gentlemen and ladies from the 1800s sitting outside in the sunshine sipping lemonade before the men did a round on the course.

This was my second time visiting the old golf course and I looked forward to getting out of the house. Jesse had done well with the client load I had left him, but sitting around the apartment watching Lana studying or go to class wasn't my style. I liked to keep busy and meeting people meant finding future clients.

Two days away from Xavier had been good for me—until he'd called me last night and left a message.

"Any valuable intel before we reach the course?" he

asked me. Just hearing his smooth voice did things to my insides in a way I didn't like.

Avoiding him or looking toward the crowd did no good. He was far taller than most of the people around us. He didn't have to work hard to look good either. He made a dark blue polo shirt and brown slacks look so stylish.

Compared to the opera, this time I was fully prepared. No emergency shopping necessary. My clothes were professional and fit in with what everyone else wore, even if they were my only set.

What I did wish that I had were shorts or slacks. My skirt revealed far too much of my legs. Xavier seemed to be looking at me every time I stole a glance his way.

"Intel, Miss Ashton?" he asked.

I'd spaced out again. "Our caddy, Luke, is already waiting for us over there. Your requested clubs are in place—"

"That I already know. What about Nakamura?"

Eager as always for the prize. "A few of Watanabe's associates will be here, but, like before, you're not here to engage Nakamura."

He slowed down a bit and I enjoyed walking side by side with him. A gentle breeze brought the scent of his cologne and I practically wanted to bathe in it. Every time I smelled him, my mind drifted back to when I'd sat on his lap at the opera house.

"Your job today is to *lose*," I added.

"Excuse me?" Amusement shined in his eyes. "Now this should be good."

"Don't get me wrong! I don't want you earning the worst stroke record for the course, but I don't want you to repeat what you did a few weeks ago." Yep, I had done my research with his assistant Ian and learned that he was just as competitive with sports as he was with his businesses.

A tall, lanky man that I recognized as Luke greeted us at the entrance to the course. Watanabe's party met us there, too. Five men, three Japanese and two Americans stood outside the door.

Everyone intermingled, exchanging bows and handshakes. This time Xavier bowed and shook hands properly with everyone. This was the real test. So far so good once our parade of carts reached the first hole. Nakamura was a bit stiff, keeping to himself, but he had greeted everyone. Most of the time he spoke Japanese with Watanabe and the two other Japanese men.

At the first hole, Xavier was to go last.

Before he played, he leaned toward my ear. My first instinct was to shift away, but I held myself in check.

"So this is where I miss a few times?" He cocked a wicked grin.

"No."

"Wild swing into the trees?"

"Don't do it."

"The water then?"

"Mr. Quinn."

"I rather like seeing you flustered. I'm going to have to do it more often."

My cheeks warmed as I watched him move to the hole. He prepared his stance and practiced his swing.

I watched the muscles in his back flex as he swung. He was powerful, practically beautiful with his technique. His first stroke went pretty far. The others murmured encouragement and remarked on his touch with the green.

As we returned to our cart, I asked, "Whatever happened to starting slow and building up?"

The look he gave me made me my heart stutter. "When there's something I want, I'm relentless from start to finish."

Xavier

As much as I was trying to impress Nakamura with my skills, or lack thereof, spending time with Sophie was pleasurable. The time went by quickly. Our conversation was casual and easy on the way to the eighth hole.

"Why aren't you playing?" I asked her when she got quiet.

"None of the assistants are playing." Her reply was nonchalant while her gaze fixed on the rolling hills of green and bunkers.

I very well knew the answer to that question, but I liked hearing her voice. She crossed her slim legs and my hungry gaze swept over them. What I wouldn't give to feel those legs wrapped around my waist, her arms linked around my neck.

"True, none of them are playing," I said, "but I wonder if you're any good."

She pursed her lips. "You're not missing anything."

"I'd like to see. You seem to be good at everything you do." *Good at driving me crazy.*

"You'd be surprised what I'm not so good at doing."

"Humor me."

She sighed, her fingers slowly intertwining in her lap. "I'm horrible at sewing, couldn't catch a ball if someone threw it into my hand, and I have this uncanny ability to run into rabid wildlife."

She smiled a bit.

"Is that it? Most people aren't good at that."

"I've sewn an arm sleeve closed before."

"I find that hard to believe. You look like the kind of woman who is good with her hands."

She rolled her eyes and snorted.

I continued. "I also find it hard to believe you didn't call me after I left that message on your phone," I added.

We approached the eighth hole as her mouth formed a straight line. "I thought it wise not to answer the call."

We pulled to a stop and joined the others. "Or listen to the message I left?" I said.

She didn't miss a beat. "I deleted it."

A grin spread into my cheeks. *Oh, yes, I loved a challenge.* Watching her walk ahead of me toward the others filled me with a familiar hunger that hadn't been satisfied since I'd gathered her in my lap at the opera house.

My eyes roamed up her long legs to the point where the hem of her golf skirt ended. While Nakamura lined up to do his shot, I stood next to her, taking in the fierceness in her eyes. Her stance was assured, but I'd glimpsed the real Sophie when I'd kissed her at the opera house. That woman looked at me with the kind of hunger that left me hopelessly hard and unable to sleep.

"So you deleted my voicemail…I rarely call women and leave messages like that," I whispered to her, but she ignored me.

I continued. "You're a professional, Miss Ashton. You'd never chance it if I had something important to say."

"I didn't delete it," she admitted.

"So did you listen to it?"

She didn't take the bait and remained silent.

"How about a friendly wager then to get things moving? If I get the shot within five paces of the hole, you'll listen to the message. If I don't then you can delete it for real."

She bit her lower lip, most likely considering my score versus Nakamura's. I was in a solid third place—a respectable gap between myself and Nakamura's second.

If I seriously reduced the strokes needed to finish this hole I'd mess with her plans.

She crossed her arms. "No deal."

I grinned, grabbing the club my caddy extended my way. "So you think I can do it."

"I didn't say that."

I loved seeing her squirm. "What kind of assistant wants to see her boss choke?"

"Fine," she whispered, "but you better adjust your score later *if* you make it."

I'd never played this course before, but golf was all about strategy and control. That was something I excelled at. I took my time with this one and studied the approach. When I caught Sophie frowning at me, I couldn't help but smile.

I feigned concern, but I didn't do it for long. I hit the ball and it landed where I expected it to: four paces from the hole. Not five like I wanted, but hey, I won the bet.

While Watanabe, and even Nakamura spoke with approval, Sophie remained silent and with crossed arms. She didn't have anything to worry about though. The next couple of holes I earned an eagle, while on some I caved into Sophie's request and underperformed. I even tossed in a bogey on the sixteenth hole.

When I fetched my ball from the sixteenth, I caught her flashing me a wide grin. Seeing her pleased expression felt good.

By the time we finished the match, I'd never had a chance to speak to Nakamura personally, but something amazing happened.

"Good game, Mr. Quinn," Nakamura said to me outside of the clubhouse. "You made me work hard today."

"Thank you, Sir," I replied. "This course has a few tricky spots."

"I'll be keeping an eye on you," was all he said after that.

After handshakes and goodbyes, he entered the club-house with his friends. That was it. There were no invites to discuss business or even share a meal. It took everything I had not to broach the subject, but I had to trust in Sophie.

Speaking of Sophie, she'd just finished chatting with my caddy and returned to my side.

Time to collect my reward.

"I believe someone lost a bet back there?" I said to her.

I'd loss the match, but I'd won something far more valuable.

With a sigh, she turned away from me to place her phone to her ear. I waited patiently, knowing very well what she was hearing.

Once she was done she didn't look my way, striding past me toward the path that led to the parking lot. "The message was...unexpected."

"And?" I caught up with her.

She paused, but kept walking. "The answer is no, Mr. Quinn."

"The reason being?" If she would've said yes to going out with me tonight, that would've been too easy.

"It's for the best that we keep things professional. You're here to conduct business with Nakamura. Not go on dates with your assistant." Her arms were crossed—almost as if she'd placed a barrier between us—but her breath had quickened. It took self-control on my part not to watch her breasts rise and fall.

Before she left my side, she had parting word. "I do

appreciate the offer and you'll be hearing from me soon on our next plan of action."

I watched her retreating back, not a bit concerned about how things were playing out so far. By the time I was done with her, she'd have absolutely no reason to say no to me.

Chapter Eleven

Sophie

I had *lied* to him about listening to the message. Right to his face in fact.

I knew very well what he'd said. Ignoring the words was easier than thinking a man like Xavier Quinn had any interest in me other than sex. Keeping that in mind made it easier for me to see him today.

I want to see you tomorrow night, he began in his lengthy message. Sleep and desire lined his words and he filled me with a need that kept me from sleeping well last night. *No strings attached,* he continued. *No entanglements. I like your company, Miss Ashton and if I have to have a casual dinner with you to accomplish it, I'm willing to do it. But be ready, when I make my move, you won't see it coming.*

His message circled like a shark in my head. Even after I deleted the voicemail for good measure. The gesture was a futile one though. He'd said the words I hadn't heard in such a long time.

The tournament today had been so much fun. He

laughed. I laughed. He'd let go and that had been refreshing. After so many instances where I had to justify saying no, the wager had caught me off guard.

No strings attached. No possible entanglements. I told myself I couldn't have a causal dinner with him though, even if it could've been a celebration for *losing*.

Instead of spending the evening alone, I called Penny and forced her to have dinner with me. I needed to have a little *chat* with her.

After texting back and forth a few times, we agreed to meet that evening at an Irish pub where Penny said the bartenders offered the best view.

I asked Lana if she wanted to join us, but the sullen look on her face told me she'd be chained to her books until the early morning.

"I'm biochemistry's bitch…" Lana groaned as I left. I nodded and offered to bring something back. Even biochemistry bitches needed love, too.

St. Dominic Place's in Restaurant Row on a Friday day was as I'd expected. I didn't have any connections here so I had to wait in line. Just like regular people.

I managed to get a table and I waited for Penny—who took her damn time to show up. "Penny time" was never everyone else's time.

By the time she showed up, I'd emptied a small basket of chips.

"What took you so long?" I asked. I was about ready to tackle any passing waiter who had food. The last waiter, a gorgeous black guy, was carrying four steaming platters of chicken pot pie and homemade chips.

"I'm might get a promotion, Soph." Delight danced in her brown eyes.

So what did a promotion in the at-home-phone sex world mean?

We ordered our food—two roasted chicken salads—

and I tried to think of how the hell I was going to broach the subject of my future participation in any of her phone calls.

So I waited until her mouth was full of food.

"There's something I wanted to discuss with you." I gathered my thoughts while I stirred the salad around. Hurting Penny's feelings wasn't my intent. "It's about this phone sex girl thing. I can't do this for you any more. I'm just not good at it."

Penny's right eyebrow rose. "Bill left you quite the tip on my account."

I shrugged.

"I bet you enjoyed it, Sophie." Her knowing smile filled her face from the top of her straight black hair to her glossy light brown lips. "Everything you'd done to Bill, someone else had done that to you."

She leaned closer as if to share a secret. "As a personal concierge, you do a great job taking care of other people. I just wished you took care of yourself too and forget about Sato."

So, it's like that? "I have."

She rolled her eyes. "What about the packages in your closet?"

"I threw away the last batch. They're all trash."

"Two of them had been opened. They had gifts and apology letters."

"Opened then trashed ." I wasn't going to discuss this topic. I *refused* to go there.

Instead of replying back to me, she glanced up as if there was someone behind me.

"What's wrong?" I turned to see Xavier standing behind me.

My heart jumped into my throat once my gaze locked with his. He was dressed in crisp white shirt and grey slacks. *What in the world was he doing here? And the next question, how long had he been standing there?*

"Mr. Quinn," I breathed.

"So did you decline my offer for dinner since you already had other plans?" He placed his warm hand on my shoulder.

I froze. Then suspicion pulsed through me. *"How did you?"*

"Lana was quite helpful."

I held in a sigh, my anger growing by the minute. Sharing my whereabouts with my clients was a no-no. All it probably took was one wink from Xavier and Lana probably fell over herself to give him my latitude and longitude coordinates.

I quickly got up and thrust my index finger at his unyielding chest. "First of all, I don't appreciate you coming here like this," I whispered.

The amused expression on his face told me he didn't care how he got here.

"My personal time is my time, Mr. Quinn and I—" A bright light flashed to my left and I turned with horror to see Penny taking our picture.

"That's what he looks like," Penny chirped into her cell. "Little Miss Thing has been keeping information from us." That little *snitch* was mostly likely on the phone with the one person I didn't want to know about Xavier yet.

Carlie.

"Who's your friend?" he asked me.

"This is Penny. We grew up together." I gestured to Xavier. "Penny this is—"

"Oh, I know who he is." Her grin widened. "What I'd like to know is how *you* know *him*?"

I opened my mouth to state my innocence, then I noticed something weird. Four couples passed me on the way to the door. Then two more. Why was everyone leaving?

"Is there an emergency?" Penny asked.

Xavier directed me, still slightly fuming, to my seat, and then he sat down in one of the free seats. "No. I just paid for a little privacy."

Penny and I glanced around. *Everyone* was leaving. There was no way he could've paid a *little* bit of money to clear out a restaurant filled with diners.

"I told you I wanted to have dinner with you, Miss Ashton. You did declined my little offer, but waiting has never been my strong point."

Across from me, Penny was beaming with amusement, giving a blow by blow to Carlie. "He had asked her out and she'd said 'no.' Unbelievable. The man is *fine* and he is dotting on her."

My face warmed and I noticed my clenched fists in my lap. The temptation to get up and leave was strong.

"Seeing as you two are nice and cozy—" Penny began.

"We are not nice and cozy. You and I were eating and chatting," I hissed.

Penny patted my shoulder on the way out. "Carlie said she'll give you a call soon. Not tonight, though. She hopes you'll be *preoccupied*."

I yelled to her back, "The next time you need a favor, Penny, I'm telling your customer that your orgasms are a recording!"

Penny simply tossed a wave over her shoulder. Lovely.

By the time the restaurant emptied to just us and the staff, I couldn't even look at him. Did he hear any of my conversation with Penny?

"You look good tonight," he finally said.

Since I was having a casual dinner with my roommate, I just wore a cream-colored sweater dress.

"Thanks," I murmured, unsure of what to say. Maybe, *I need to leave*. Or perhaps, *you've crossed the line, Mr. Quinn*.

But also the very idea of getting up bothered me, too. I placed my hand on my clutch purse, but I didn't pick it up. I missed going out for reasons other than business.

If I stayed though, what did all this mean? My grip on my bag tightened.

"Stay," was all he said.

It wasn't a request. It was a command that flowed over me like silk over pebbled nipples.

I let go of the purse and placed my hands in my lap. "Fine."

Time stretched out a bit. The intensity of his gaze made it hard for me to focus. We were face to face again with unsaid words hovering around us. *What does this date mean? How can you go on a date with someone you're attracted to without thinking of something more?*

"Surprised you don't have more to say to me. You were so chatty during the golf tournament," he remarked. "You're quiet now."

Right now he'd caught me off guard. I worked crowds. Having him all to myself was another deal. I crossed and re-crossed my legs. Maybe I even licked my lips for a third time.

"You don't need my help tonight," I managed. "I guess I'm without words. Is there something you'd like to ask me right now?"

He shook his head and the waiter appeared.

"Anything I can offer the lady of the evening to drink?" the thick-set, tattooed man offered.

Xavier glanced my way and tilted his head. "May I offer a suggestion?"

"Sure."

"Two Cusqueñas please."

The waiter nodded. "Good choice."

Once the waiter left, Xavier picked up his chair and brought it over to my side of the table. It felt strange to be honest. Sitting next to him side by side in a pub.

"You're like a mouse caught in a trap. I like that. What's on your mind?" he finally asked.

"You want the truth?"

"I wouldn't ask otherwise."

"Why did you come here?" Might as well get to the point.

His smile widened. "I asked myself the same thing." He placed the tip of his finger under my chin and pulled up so that I met his gaze. "The answer was simple: I couldn't find a reason not to see you more."

I melted into his light blue eyes every single time he discussed logic and reason. Hadn't he said what was happening between us was inevitable? Did that mean I was practically lining up for disappointment the day he walked out the door?

"True."

His hand drifted down my cheek, over to my arm, and then my wrist. Goosebumps formed where he touched me.

"I'd like to get to know you better, Sophie."

"What do you want to know?"

He shrugged. "You said you travel a lot. Tell me more."

He finally coaxed a smile out of me. "I leave the US a lot more than I used to. Now I have to explore sites for my clients, but I'd like to travel to enjoy things like regular people. See the cheesy tourist spots instead of the exclusive clubs. Buy cheap knockoff souvenirs instead of bobbles and such that nobody could ever afford." My hand went up to defend my last statement. "Not that I don't like shiny stuff, but I've grown up with less, and I've learned that the most valuable thing to have is connections and not possessions."

"Connections?" His hand continued to rest on my wrist and I wanted to squirm from the closeness. His knee rested against mine and my concentration faltered.

"Back before I did this line of work, I was a secretary at a hotel in New York City. Not a bad job, but I was damn good at it. I could talk to anyone and I made customer satisfaction look easy." I smiled from the old memories. That was a great time for me. The world had possibilities and I was hungry to explore them.

"As much as I loved NYC, Carlie was in Boston and I missed her so I relocated here. My best friend got me my first concierge client and after that, as they say, is ancient history. Since that point, I've been collecting connections."

"So you're practically a LinkedIn website waiting to happen?"

I chuckled. "You could say that."

His eyes met mine and I looked away again. This connection between us made my breath hitch and my heart beat faster.

We chatted for a bit and I enjoyed his company.

Soon enough, more food arrived to replace the salads I ate with Penny. We ate roasted chicken breast sandwiches and handmade potatoes chips. Everything was filling and the beer kept coming. Beer from Germany, Netherlands, Peru, and even a malt liquor from Japan.

"Are you trying to get me drunk?" I wasn't tipsy, but a pleasant buzz whirled through me.

"Not in the least," his reply was smooth. "We can stop if you like? Whenever I'm overseas I prefer these. I thought you'd like them."

Our waiter appeared and took our plates. Xavier beckoned the man and he leaned toward the waiter's ear and whispered. Without a word, the waiter headed to the far wall and began typing into the jukebox on the wall. Additional waiters cleared a few tables out of the way to make space. A slow song from John Mayer began to play.

He looked at me then I looked up at him.

He cocked his head in question and I tried to look away with a growing smile. "One dance, Miss Ashton. Especially if this is as close as I'm going to get to holding you tonight."

So he didn't want more from me tonight other than dinner and a dance? I followed him to the cleared out space. The moment he wrapped his arms around me, I sighed.

"I thought this would be easy," he whispered into my ear. "Come find you. Have a few drinks. Eat a casual dinner. But you feel so good." His hand drifted over my back and settled right over my bottom. The curve of my body settled against his and I closed my eyes. He was right, this did feel good.

We settled into a slow rhythm as John's words folded over us. The sway allowed me to rest my forehead against his shoulder. The rapid thumps of his heartbeat thudded against my cheek. I wanted to open my eyes and look up. To surrender to what I really wanted. This wasn't fair. It was too easy to want him. This itch inside of me could be scratched. This yearning could be quelled and tomorrow I might feel whole again instead of empty.

Being lonely was a tiring affair.

I opened my mouth to speak. I had to say something to pull myself out of the moment. "Do you feel more comfortable now about meeting Nakamura face-to-face?" I managed. "Need any tips?"

"There are things you need to teach me," he admitted.

I didn't roll my eyes this time, but I was sure he caught

my amusement. "There are books. Youtube videos. A Japanese protocol person. You could buy Youtube, couldn't you?"

"Books don't have that *personal* touch." He traced a circle along the middle of my back, making my stomach jump. My grip on his shoulders tightened.

"Do you need anything?" he asked.

Need. Such a simple word that didn't convey my thoughts. *Crave.* Now that better served the purpose. "Yes, I need more," I whispered in a way that betrayed my true thoughts. "I've been waiting for more."

His blue eyes darkened and I froze. He edged me toward the table until the back of my thighs hit. His rough breath warmed my cheek. Teasingly close to my mouth. Then his lips captured mine. He kissed me so hard I couldn't hold myself up and my knees buckled a bit. I was so enraptured I couldn't hold back the moan in the back of my throat. By the time we parted he was breathing just as hard as I was.

"Damn it, Soph." His grip on my hips hardened and I wished we were truly alone.

I reached for him and we kissed again. Every wall I had built to separate us crumbled. This felt right. My lips against his. The tentative brush of my tongue along his. Velvety soft would be the best way to describe the way his tongue felt while he gently rocked his hips against mine. We settled into a rocking motion, rocking forward, tongue dip, then upward stroke of his hips. Almost as if our clothes didn't hinder what we truly wanted to do.

His hands left my hips to travel over my stomach, stopping briefly to rub along my waist. His fingertips brushed against my breasts and I had to swallow another pleasurable moan. Then he reached for my face and cupped my cheeks.

"If you only knew what I want to do to you, Sophie." I loved hearing him say my name. His deep voice was honeyed with desire and the dark dare in his eyes made me want to find out exactly what he'd do to me.

"Please kiss me again," I whispered.

He leaned in to draw his tongue across my parted lips. My inner thighs quivered and the heat gathering there told me if he ripped off my panties he'd find me wet and ready for him. Would he fuck me on this very table if I asked him?

He pressed me closer to him, drawing my bottom onto the table.

A dropped glass from the kitchen nearby drew him away from me.

"Don't like giving a show?" I quipped.

"I could give them a show, but I don't know if you're the quiet type or a screamer."

If he only knew what I really wanted to do with him. Was he even the type? We'd never had such a talk yet. Everything between us was so new. Was he an exhibitionist? Had he ever been in a Dominant/submissive relationship? Was he into kink?

Those weren't on my new client questionnaire, by the way...

"Let's get out of here." He picked up my clutch and offered it to me.

By the time we reached outside, I finally asked where we were going. Were we going back to his place?

"I'm not done dancing with you yet," he replied to me.

Xavier

This early in the evening, finding a dance club in Boston wasn't hard. Even I knew where to look for a dark place with a VIP section for us.

As much as I wanted Sophie in my bed, I was playing things by ear. She gave every sign she wanted me to make the first move, but I was in no hurry.

Just because she wore wrist cuffs didn't mean she had the same kinky interests as me. They might've been a fashion statement. As much as I wanted to dominate Sophie, she wasn't Rosalie, nor did I expect her to be. The games I preferred to play were unusual.

When we got into the car, she slid in beside me. The need to turn to her and gather her onto my lap flicked at me, but I didn't so much as move. If the opportunity presented itself, I'd show her what I wanted.

By the time we found a spot in VIP section at the Viper Bar, I was pleased with my decision to have drinks first. During the whole time, I watched her movements. The way she left a few inches of space between us. Close, but not close enough for me to touch her. The way she tried to hold back her coy smile whenever she snuck a gaze my way. She had no expectations for conversation and I appreciated that. All the stressors from thinking about securing the deal from Nakamura melted away for a moment.

When she briefly excused herself to use the bathroom, I got a chance for a breather. Until I saw a man stop her on her way back. He was some dude who looked like he was athlete or something. I knew the type. Wide shoulders, thick chest from exercise. I bet this guy expected women to flock to him whenever he flashed his big bank account.

Darkness gathered in my chest when he leaned toward her to speak. She briefly pointed my way to show where she was heading, but he stopped her to point back to the bar downstairs from the VIP section. He wanted to dance with her.

When he placed his hand on her back, I got up. She might be my assistant, but I invited her here and this guy wasn't taking up *my time*.

I approached them and she turned to me.

"Is there a problem, Sophie?" I asked.

She shook her head. I exchanged a glance at the guy. If a pissing match could've occurred, I was sure we would've done it.

"Is this your date?" the guy asked.

"She's with me tonight, yes." I didn't hesitate.

"My bad. I didn't want such a pretty lady drinking by herself tonight."

I'm sure you didn't, pal, I thought.

I didn't stop myself when I placed my hand around her waist and tugged her closer to me. The guy nodded and backed away.

At my side Sophie had a half-grin.

"Do you know him?" I asked. I had to lean in close for her to hear me.

"Not really. He recognized me from a party I attended a few weeks ago."

We slid into the private booth. I scooted in until the shadows hid me.

"He seemed pretty interested in you." I pulled her toward me until she edged on to my lap. Might as well make it easier to have conversation.

"I haven't had a chance to speak with him personally. Never hurts to be friendly."

"But he liked you." And I didn't *like* that.

"And?" Her eyebrows rose.

"You're here with me."

Her lips pursed and I knew what was coming. It still bothered me nonetheless.

"Aren't we just getting to know each other tonight?"

Good try, sweetheart. No dice. "I don't share, Sophie." I *never* shared. Not even Rosalie.

"People in relationships don't share, but I'm just your assistant, right?"

I did know enough about her to consider her an acquaintance, but tonight I wanted much more than that. Damn it, I wanted to show every man who stared at her that she was with me and no one else could touch her.

But she was right. Even I'd told her I didn't want relationship and I'd meant it. That still didn't stop my growing need to be with her.

"Yes, we have a business relationship," I said crisply.

"Glad to hear that's settled." She pushed her drink my way, but I didn't touch it. "You like beer, well I like Sex on the Beach. Want a sip?"

I chuckled a bit, enjoying the coy look in her eyes.

"I prefer harder liquors. Do you like those, too?"

"Just once in a while. After too many tequila shots, my friends once had to use a spatula to scrape me off the floor."

She sipped her drink and we watched the small dance floor in the VIP section. The pounding rhythm of the house music flowed through me. A couple, a small blonde and a dude in black, near us got up to dance.

Sophie pressed her back to my chest as we watched the woman sway her hips to the music. The dreamy look on the blonde's face was hypnotic. My left hand drifted along Sophie's hip down her thigh. From her knee I traveled up her thighs to press my hand to the warm space under her breasts. Her heartbeat thundered against my hand. The need to cup her beautiful breasts made me thrust upward, and she responded in kind, grinding her ass against my lap.

I gently pushed her forward, placing her hands on the small table in front of us to brace herself, then I ran my hands down her back as she rocked her hips against me. Damn, she felt so good. Tension filled my hips as my shaft turned to steel and my balls clenched tight enough to hurt.

"Stop," I commanded.

My hands locked around her hips to hold her in place. When the need to come backed up off a bit, I eased up, but she didn't start moving again.

She waited, her body trembling as if she was on the edge of a cliff needing to be pushed off urgently. Was she an instrument needing to be played? A fine instrument with a tune needing to be heard? *But would she be willing to do what I ordered her to do to give her pleasure?*

I had particular tastes: The main one being control. As a Dom I knew what I wanted, and I needed for her to trust in the pleasure I wanted to give her.

My fingers trailed along her thigh. Once I reached her inner thighs, I paused.

Lord almighty, she was soaking wet.

She twisted to look at me. I looked at her.

One thing became abundantly clear: *Tonight wasn't going to end as a casual date.*

Chapter Twelve

Sophie

The dark look on Xavier's face scorched me to the point where I had to look away. But turning away from him didn't end his visual assault. He pulled me back against his chest again, decreasing the distance between us until his breath warmed my cheek.

His mouth brushed against my ear. A light, teasing touch. As he rested his fingertips on my thigh, he spoke. "I want you and I can promise no entanglements. The next step isn't mine to take, but yours. Go to Fenway Park nearby. There's a small grove not far from an ice cream stand. Rest your hands against a fence to a small garden. Wait for me. Don't move."

Then he placed me next to him and got out of the booth. He left the club, leaving me there to contemplate the bomb he'd left in my lap. All this time I wouldn't have imagined he'd say such a thing. In all the research I'd done, I never read anything about Xavier Quinn being kinky.

And yet, he was.

Also, he hadn't given me an order like Sato, but a choice. It was my choice to follow him outside and wait.

As much as I thought he'd given me a choice, the cadence to his voice had carried a command. Just the thought of going outside made my breath quicken even further, but it was up to me if I wanted to do it. To saunter across the line he'd placed in the sand.

As I slowly got up on wobbly legs, I considered what he said to me. I didn't have to go—I could take a cab home and forget we'd ever reached this point, but there was something in his eyes I hadn't seen in a long time. A promise of passion *and* pleasure. He wanted to be with me right now. That was something I'd never shared with Sato. No scheduled visit via text or a phone message.

I left the club.

Once I was at the curb, my decision was clear. I let the cabs pass and I headed down Bolyston Street toward the Fenway Park.

The spring night had a cool breeze that fluttered through my hair and added confidence to my step. I looked around for Xavier but didn't see him anywhere. The park was at the end of the street—the first sign of trees lay two blocks ahead. With each step, apprehension circled my stomach. Countless questions came to mind, but I batted them away.

What the hell are you doing, Sophie?

Good question. *You're about to get off, girlfriend.*

Are you prepared to sleep with your employer?

Yep. *You don't have to do anything you don't want to do, but if you want to fuck him until you climax hard enough to have a concussion that is your right in the good 'ole US of A.*

So I marched down to Fenway Park and I found the closed-up ice cream stand as he directed. From there it was a bit hard to find the grove, but once I found the cluster of trees protecting it, locating the garden was easy.

And what a garden it was.

In the moonlight, I could make out every white lilies leaning over as if in prayer. Fragrant, yellow evening prim-rose that appeared almost purple at night.

All of them were night-blooming flowers.

I placed my hands on the fence as instructed, a thrill dancing down my spine. The need to look around pecked at me, but I was always obedient at this game.

A minute passed and when I clenched my thighs, my wetness was apparent. I was soaked.

As I waited, my anticipation grew to the point where the sounds of the crickets and night birds drowned out the sound of my beating heart.

My grip on the metal fence tightened.

Wait. Don't Move.

Then I sensed him behind me. Closing my eyes, I waited for him. Yearned for him to do what he promised.

"I'm going to touch you," Xavier murmured.

"Yes," I breathed. He hadn't asked. He'd told me so. I wanted him to touch me. Needed him to brush his full lips against mine. Lock my hands over my head as he took what he wanted.

His head dipped to the crook of my neck, his lips resting near my pulse point. His warm breath against my neck made my breath hitch in response. Any minute now a frenzy would hit. The tension in my stomach grew tighter.

He knelt behind me, his hands running down my body. His fingertips caressed my knee toward the sensitive skin along my inner thigh. His other hand stretched across my belly to my hip. He tugged me to spread my legs wider.

"That's it, sweetheart." His voice was thick as he stood again. The chain link fence moaned as he pressed me against it. His erection was hot against my bottom. There was no escape. He leaned in to nibble along the heated skin at the crook of my neck.

"I want to kiss you again so badly," he said. His tongue darted out to trace a circle, and then his lips slowly kissed the spot. I melted in his arms. "You taste good. Like strawberries."

I reached for him, but the hand on my hip grabbed my wrists and forced me to keep my hands on the fence.

Naughty, naughty Sophie. I already forgot my orders.

"That's not what I want tonight, Miss Ashton," he said with a husky chuckle.

I found that hard to believe. His hips thrust upwards against my ass and I couldn't resist squirming.

"So what do you—" I began.

"Don't speak," he said firmly.

I swallowed down any replies I had. I rather liked this game and was eager to comply.

His heated right hand caressed my thigh over my clothes. Heading upward he drifted until his fingertips dipped down the apex of my legs, effectively brushing against my mound. The stretchy material didn't resist his manipulation and I shuddered, unable to respond in kind. If my hands were free, I'd be running them through his hair. All over his wide chest. I wanted to turn around and face him, but he didn't budge.

He rubbed me again, going from my clit down to my entrance, much faster this time. A throaty moan escaped my mouth. Why couldn't he yank up my dress? He was so teasingly close.

"Are you still wet?" he asked.

I remembered what he told me earlier and nodded instead of speaking.

"I don't believe you." He laughed against my cheek. "I should make sure you're not lying to me."

He thrust upwards. Two quick pulses of his hips. The hard outline of his erection against my pussy made the growing need inside me intensify. Damn, it felt so good.

"You're going to come for me right now. As much as I'd like to fuck you all night in my bed, all I need tonight is to feel you against me when you let go."

His movements quickened as he pulled up my dress. The damp, silk panties should've come off, too, but they didn't. Instead he left them in place and slid two fingers between my pussy lips and slipped them into my channel. My thighs clenched. His ragged breath fanned my neck. "Nice and wet. I'll have to taste that some time."

He pulled out and pushed into me again with three fingers this time. I almost gasped out his name. My hands formed fists on the fence. The flowers before me blurred and my eyes formed slits. He thrust into me again. In and out. Out and in. He settled into rhythm, driving me crazy since I couldn't cry out.

"I wanna hear you come now." His grip around my waist tightened. The constraint was delicious. "Does it feel good?"

The building moan inside me stretched out as he pistoned my panties into me.

"That's right. Come for me."

I cried out. I had no choice but to comply.

As sweet pleasure washed over me, my back arched, my stomach clenched, and everything in me tensed up. The moment had to have lasted a few seconds, but it felt far longer than that.

Finally, my back collapsed against his chest and every burden I had faded away.

I was still slightly bent over the fence. My boss's arm was still wrapped around me.

So what happens now? I wasn't sure what to say.

A breeze stirred the flowers. In the very back was a small *gekka bijin*, a *beauty under the moon* as Sato had called me. A stark reminder that I'd bloomed tonight, but in the morning I'd have to close my petals again.

Time for the real world to come crashing down on us.

I took a step to the side. He closed back in. As much as I hated to admit it, if he took me in his arms right now I'd go wherever he led.

But when I took another two steps, he took one.

"Are you all right?" he asked softly.

I managed a nod.

No entanglements. A simple request he was able to fulfill.

"I should get going now," was what I managed to say as I adjusted my clothes. Saying less meant less conversation.

I left the grove. If we went together, I'd have to face him while I got a cab or I'd have to decline his offer for a ride home.

He promised no entanglements, and yet he followed me back to the road. I hailed a cab and got inside.

I closed my eyes to avoid the temptation of looking out the window to see him standing there. It was for the best. I'd done what I'd needed to do. I'd sate the hunger within me. Quite well, thank you very much.

But even if I were satisfied tonight, what would tomorrow bring with a man like Xavier Quinn?

THE MORNING after a long night of partying can be a

rough one. Yet, this time was different. I wasn't lying on my side.

My drawer was shut. Still nice and locked away.

I picked up my phone and went through the overnight messages.

Not a single one from Xavier. Good.

Not that I was checking.

Once I was done, I stretched out on the bed. Every muscle from my legs to my arms was blissfully relaxed. I even probably smiled like a damn fool. The fingers on my right hand ran along the edge of my left hand's wrist cuff. The worn leather was smooth.

Carefully, I took them off. A long shower this morning would do me good.

I was almost to the shower when my phone buzzed. A call from a client around 7:30 a.m. seemed a bit early. Usually Jesse took care of anything that came up overnight.

It was a call from Carlie.

"What you up to, C?" I asked softly.

"You sound cheerful. It's practically the ass crack of dawn there."

I laughed. "If your clients knew how you sounded when you talked to your friends…"

"They'd be horrified, yes, but only my true friends know my *secret* identity."

I sat on my bed. "And you only have so many of those."

"I need to be that way in the business we're in. I can't make mistakes anymore."

"K," was all I said. Mentioning Carlie's past flame wasn't done between us.

"Yep." She was quick to add, "So did you sleep in after your little *date*? I've never seen you sleep more than four hours or so."

I should've seen this coming. I rarely kept secrets from her. "I was reading." Technically, I was reading my phone.

"Bullshit. Who reads cookbooks in bed?"

I rolled my eyes.

"When were you going to tell me about tall, dark, and fuckable?" Her tone was teasing, but sweet.

I chewed on my bottom lip. "It's complicated—and no I haven't fucked him yet."

"I see." She paused for a bit and I knew what was coming. "Do you like him?"

I was quick to reply. "We just met a few days ago and he's not looking for anything serious."

"So you do like him!"

"Oh, Carlie, stop it."

"I distinctly remember you giving me the same sorry ass response when I asked you about Robert Graham."

I groaned. "That was high school and now that I think about it, I have no idea why I found that guy attractive." Memories of Robert's stark red hair, massive braces and pimply face came to mind. "Oh my God, his hair. It was redder than yours! And I've never seen a tongue that big before."

"You were tangling with that tongue at every opportunity." Carlie laughed, then sighed. She never liked being a ginger and dyed her hair all the time.

Reminiscing was always fun with Carlie, but unease settled into my stomach—we flat out avoided talking about hers. In particular, the one person she didn't want to think about.

So I finally said it. "I wonder how Tomas is doing sometimes."

"*I don't.*"

For one summer back when we were sixteen, Carlie and I met a rich kid visiting from the UK. Back when we'd first met him, all we saw was a guy in worn jeans and T-shirts with a golden smile. A hint of an accent when he spoke. We had no idea he was the son of a man who owned a bunch of luxurious hotels.

Back then the conditions of our foster home had been pretty shitty. Our foster parent Gail barely clothed and fed us—instead taking the money the state gave for our care toward her gambling habit. Before Gail, our lives had been so much better, but life never goes the way you want. The memories kept flooding my senses and I stamped down the ones that left me bitter. What I did try to recall was that particular summer. The smile that Tomas had that was reflected in Carlie.

A few years later we were eighteen and on our own during another hot NYC summer. Even with opened windows, the sweltering heat turned breathing an Olympic event. But that was our lot in life. That dirty studio apartment was all Carlie and I could afford in Queens, so we endured the heat as best we could.

Not long into the summer the worst bit of news fell at our feet: An eviction notice was posted to our door. We ignored it as long as we could until the final notice came. Move out tomorrow or the police would come.

"You look like shit," Carlie had said to me that morning with a smirk.

My clothes clung to me, wet with perspiration. "You stink."

"Your comeback stinks." We always did this to distract each other when the other person was about to crash.

Which I was about to do right now. My fingers gripped the paper hard enough to make the material crackle. My nose grew stuffy and I was unable to stop a tear from falling.

"Don't you dare cry, Ashley," Carlie bit out. "This is just another piece of shit apartment."

I shook my head with a dry laugh. I hated when she called me by my birth name. Yep, I was born Ashley Ashton. The double Ash got on my nerves once in a while. When she really wanted to dig under my skin, she used Ash Ashton.

When I got the money, I was changing my first name to my middle one. *When I get money…* At the very thought of cash, my stomach muscles tightened to the point of pain. We were beyond broke. I wouldn't be changing my name any time soon.

Not far from me, Carlie's foot tapped against the worn floor. She stared out the only window we had—which offered a wonderful view of a crumbling brick wall.

Somehow I got up and strode to the kitchenette area. Tears continued to fall and I ignored them as best as I could. From under the sink, I plucked the few garbage bags we had.

All the while I couldn't stop wondering about where we'd go. *Another shelter?* They'd be packed in this heat. Maybe one of our friends would let us sleep on the floor. One quick side-glance at Carlie told me, she'd vote down that idea. She'd always hated getting charity.

"Handouts are for people who really need them," she'd always say to me. *"What I need is to earn my way."*

Watching Carlie stare out the window at the expansive brick scenery wouldn't keep our landlord from tossing our clothes on the street, so I went to our scratched up dresser and opened the first drawer.

"Sit down, Soph," Carlie said to my back.

"Why?" When I turned around, Carlie had discarded her shirt and shorts. "What are you doing?"

She fished out a red dress—the color was faded to a

muted maroon—from the dresser. "What needs to be done."

"We aren't whores!" I grabbed her arm to stop her.

"I'm going to see him."

Oh, hell no. I shook my head. "Not today. Not ever again."

Carlie brushed back her dampened red hair, determination in every sharp movement. "I don't care. We're not waiting in the heat to be turned away from a shelter."

I tried to hide her purse, but she snatched it out of my hands.

"Sophie. Let me go." She stroked my cheeks in same way she did when we were kids. The touch calmed me each time. "I let him go once before. I can do it again."

She tilted her head and gave me a bright smile. The sprinkle of freckles on her cheeks made her bright red hair all the more endearing, but a part of her faded away the last time she'd left Tomas behind. Our lives were as intertwined with his as much as he was with us. Their paths crossed again and again as if their very existence together was defined by serendipity.

"It's simple. I'll ask him for the money and he'll help us out of this mess." But as she walked out of the apartment, I knew love was never that simple.

Our rent money came via courier an hour later and my best friend came back in tears a few months later.

Our silence stretched out for a bit as the memories from that day faded away. Perhaps she was thinking about Tomas, too. I heard clicks from her keyboard. It was afternoon in the UK. She was probably at her office handling emails and such.

I was waiting for her to nag me about Xavier—maybe even about moving to the UK, but she didn't. The silence stretched to painful levels.

"Everything OK?" I asked.

"No, it's not." She sucked in a breath.

"What's going on?"

"I found them, Soph."

Her birth parents.

Last year I'd conducted a similar search, but I'd turned up nothing. Compared to Carlie, I'd come to terms with the fact that when my mother had left me at the hospital after giving birth to me, she hadn't meant to take me with her or ever be found. Case closed.

"I've got their address in Boston right here. They must've left NY after I was born." The sound of her gripping the paper bled through the phone. "After I learned their names, a friend helped me get an address."

I nodded, even though she couldn't see the gesture.

"I'm scared, Soph. When there's something I want, I get it, but I'm *regretting* this for once."

"You're the strongest person I know. You'll be fine." I sighed. "It's just a place to visit. You could even use a third party to make the initial introductions."

Envy briefly made me pause, but I kept going. I had to be there for Carlie. "If you want I can go there for you. Maybe setup a lunch before you fly here."

"I'm not ready yet. I don't think I'll ever be. I have so much to do and these new distractions are killing me." She groaned.

"Don't say that." This wasn't the woman I knew who pushed me to do better. To expect better.

"I wish you were here," she admitted.

"I wish I was, too. We'd be having a late lunch and you could get caught up on all my adventures." Xavier's name sat on the tip of my tongue, but I didn't say his name. Now wasn't the time to talk about what I faced.

"You always make things better, Soph. I can't be strong

all the time and having you as a part of my team would really help me get through this."

I almost said yes right then and there. It would make things easier to just give in. And yet… There was a yet.

"As much as I'd like to be there for you right now, I can't leave any time soon. I've got a huge client who needs my help to secure an important contract."

"Of course. Of course. Our clients come first." She drew in a long breath. "Look, take care of them. Wrap things up and then really give some thought about coming to London. You wouldn't have to worry about a place to stay or anything like that."

"Thanks."

I ended the phone call with a promise she'd tell me when she made plans to contact her parents. I wanted to hear all the details and support her if things didn't go well.

As I got up and headed to the shower, I told myself I was dragging my feet because I liked Xavier's company. He got what he wanted and I got what I wanted.

When I looked in my bathroom mirror, the woman who looked back at me had a shine in her eyes and she parted her lips as if in anticipation of good things to come.

"A girlfriend is the last thing I'm looking for," he'd said.

He was practically telling me to move away.

Chapter Thirteen

Xavier

No entanglements. That was what I'd said to Sophie, so why did I go to bed every night and wake up still thinking about her? Even the gym didn't help this morning. Today the place was packed on a weekend, everyone determined to do their time and escape back to the land of the living.

I, for one, had trouble getting through each set. What happened to us played over and over again in my mind: from dinner, to the club, and then our encounter in the park.

While I ran on the treadmill, I couldn't stop remembering the taste of her lips. While I worked myself to a drenched sweat on the wide-grip lat pulldown, her smell made it hard for me to focus. And when I finally gave in to do free weights, thinking I'd purge myself of distractions, I drowned myself in the pleasure I experienced as I finger-fucked her in the park. Her soft sounds permeated my senses, leaving my dick perpetually hard and eager to feel her under me.

"We have another opportunity to meet Nakamura. Don't be late to the teahouse, this evening," the text message from her read.

Now there was the stiff Sophie I was expecting this morning. Not a single phone call since that night. Only text messages. After what happened between us, I expected as much.

Well, I wasn't letting her have all the fun trying adding a gulf between us. Right after my shower, I hurried through my morning business then I marched right over to her place.

Around eleven, the area was pretty packed for a nearby farmer's market. Chris couldn't park nearby so I walked a few blocks to reach her door. The walk was nice and cleared my thoughts as I climbed to the second level of her apartment building.

After a few knocks, a short redhead, who I remembered as Lana, answered the door and stared at me with bleary eyes. "Can I help you?"

She squinted. "You look familiar."

I stuffed my hands in my pockets, asked for Sophie, and briefly re-introduced myself.

"Oh, yeah, I remember you…Just a sec." Then she closed the door on me.

Now this was something new. The last time I knocked on someone's door was post-college. I couldn't help grinning.

The door opened not long after she closed it with a lovely, yet disgruntled Sophie.

"Miss Ashton," I said softly.

Gone was the makeup and finely coiffed hair. Her dark hair lay in gentle waves along her shoulders and she looked incredibly sexy in a Red Sox T-shirt and cut-off shorts.

The real Sophie Ashton stood before me.

"What are you doing here?" she asked.

"I stopped by to discuss a few things before we meet later."

"Sophie, is he coming in?" Lana whispered from behind her.

"Good morning," I called out. I took the opportunity to walk past Sophie into the apartment. Last time I was here, when I found out where Sophie was eating dinner, I never got a chance to see her home.

"It's rather early, Mr. Quinn," Sophie said.

"It's almost noon," I quipped. "You must think I'm still on west coast time." This time I saw her third roommate, the beautiful Indian woman she called Penny from the other night. The other two ladies were all smiles as I took in the living room. What I could see of the place anyway. The windows out to the street let in a lot of light and revealed the sheer messiness of the place. I had to watch where I stepped to avoid mountains of textbooks and papers.

"Sorry about that," Lana said as she tried to clear the hardwood floor. "I pulled an overnighter for the test I have on Monday."

The redhead's smile widened and she tried to smooth over her wrinkled *Nirvana* T-shirt. "I don't like to study at a desk. I'm a free-thinker who wanders as I work. Small crammed spaces inhibit higher forms of learning."

"*I see…*" I said. She was dead serious.

Sophie hid her mortification with lowered eyebrows. "I'm just glad you haven't tried naked-studying like you promised us last semester." She turned to me. "If you'll give me a moment, I'll go get my purse."

Before I even had a chance to settle into a chair—once Lana removed some notebooks to make it possible to sit—Sophie had emerged from her room in a dark blue, knee-length summer dress, heeled sandals, and a purse. She wasn't wearing her leather cuffs today.

That had to be a world record of some kind. Didn't women have to do some kind of makeup routine and their hair? Apparently, Sophie didn't need such frivolities. Her face was fresh and she'd left her hair down. I couldn't stop staring at her. She looked good.

She glanced at me over her shoulder on the way to do the door. "Are you coming, Mr. Quinn?"

I said my goodbyes to Lana and Penny and followed her out. With amusement I chuckled when I had to hurry after her down the stairs.

"Why did you change?" I asked.

She tried to hide her amusement, but made a small *tsk* noise instead. "When I'm with my clients I dress this way. You're here really early." She sighed. "We shouldn't be alone like this."

"I'm not wasting an opportunity with Nakamura. I want to be ready for anything." Chris wasn't waiting for us outside so directed her toward Orleans Street, which was less crowded with traffic.

She had a slight hesitation to her step, but kept going down Maverick Street.

"Busy day," she murmured.

"I passed a farmer's market. You had anything to eat this morning?"

"I had coffee."

"Which isn't breakfast. How do you function?"

"On fumes most of the time."

My knee kicked in a bit, with a familiar ache, but I ignored it and kept up with her. "We can walk and talk. Discuss business."

"Seemed like we did enough *talking* the other night."

Just seeing her lips part and her sharp inhale made me

think about how well the dress fit over the curve of her back and her breasts.

We walked a past apartment buildings and small businesses. The street widened until we reached the farmer's market. For three blocks, the market cut off through traffic. Many shoppers were here and they forced her to stand closer to me. She didn't back away when I placed my hand on the small of her back to get out of the way of a mother pushing a stroller with two kids.

"So where to?" I asked.

"You ever been to one of these things before?"

"To be honest, not in a long time. My grandfather, back when he was alive, used to do this kind of thing to sell the food he grew in his backyard."

She nodded while I spoke. We continued down the street deeper into the market.

"What did he sell?" she asked.

"All sort of things. Peaches. Apples. Those grow pretty well in southern California."

"I thought you lived in Arizona?"

"He lived there. When my dad started the resort business, he founded his company outside of Phoenix."

We approached a woman selling coffee and pastries. I asked Sophie if this looked good.

"Smells great." She chose a puff pastry.

I also bought us two coffees. By the time our hands were full, Sophie was eating and I was watching her smile while she ate. The booths seemed nice and others tried to get our attention to stop by, but we kept going. She finished her food, but she had a piece of pastry on her cheek. I brushed it away and she flinched. Not good.

"You told me the other day there'd be no strings attached," she whispered.

"A few things have changed," I replied.

She didn't respond. I tried to read her expression, but couldn't.

So I continued. "And yet some things haven't. I'm still here to secure that contract. After I'm done, I'm going back to Arizona." I wouldn't get attached to her like I did Rosalie. Sophie and I knew from the start where this was going. We should enjoy the time we had before I leave.

A hint of a smile touched her lips. "So why complicate things between us?"

"Because I want you. We have unfinished business." I stopped in the middle of the sidewalk while others flowed around us. With all the noise, she was forced to stand close to me. Her hazel eyes blinked rapidly and the rapid rise and fall of her chest spoke volumes.

"This won't end well if we keep going on like this," she whispered.

"We're both adults. We know what we want. I know what you need and you know what I want. What's so complicated about that?"

Her tongue darted out to lick her bottom lip. The need to kiss her nipped at me. Would she taste like the strawberries on the puff pastry she'd eaten?

"We shouldn't do this, Xavier. Relationships can still get weird. Matter of fact, maybe I should ask point blank what you want from me? Do you want a Dominant/submissive relationship? Or maybe a girlfriend?"

At the mention of my name, my heartbeat sped up. Her voice was soft and slid over me like her hands sliding over my body. "I do know I'm not ready for a sub or a girlfriend. I'd like to see what happens naturally."

"What happens if one of us wants to end our arrangement and the other person doesn't?"

"As long as we acknowledge this is temporary, there will always be an out. If you tell me you don't want me, I'll respect that." I ran the tips of my fingers over the buttery smooth skin along her jaw. She shuddered from my touch.

She shook her head a bit as if trying to convince herself of something. "This isn't a good idea. Is this what you do with other women?" Her attempt to sound like she was making a joke didn't go well. "Spend a few days with them, then move onto the next one?"

"No, I don't." I placed my hand on her back and we started moving again. "Like I said before, most of the time, the women I'm photographed with are dates. They go out with me to be seen and that's it." She didn't need to ever know I'd considered loving a woman forever.

By the time the farmer's market ended, I pondered her silence. The feel of her body next to mine felt good. I almost wanted to walk slower instead of faster. The moment she'd get into my car, she'd slid across the seat and we'd be back to where we were before. In that moment, I knew two headstrong people would just bounce back and forth. She wanted hard facts. Was I willing to seal the deal? I wrestled with my thoughts until I came to a decision.

"What if I was open to seeing what happens before I secure my contract?" I asked.

She stopped and we turned to face each other.

"What do you want to happen?"

I want to touch you everywhere, I thought. *I want to hear you call my name as I crash through all the walls you've built around yourself to keep me out. By the time I'm done with you, all those lonely feelings you have trapped inside won't be there anymore.*

Instead of saying those things, I whispered, "We have unfinished business, Sophie and the only way to finish is to come to an agreement."

"Then what have we agreed to do?"

"We've agreed to see where this takes us. Entangle-ments or not."

She slowly nodded with a hint of a smile. "I'm not sure about a few things, but what I do know is that standing with you right now is something I can agree to do."

Anticipation made the muscles along my stomach jump. "Then let's see what happens."

TONIGHT WAS the opportunity I'd been waiting for since I'd arrived in Boston. A face-to-face encounter with the very man I wanted to see. I had an invite from Nakamura himself to attend a dinner at Sakura No Hana with him and his assistant.

And yet, as I stood outside of the teahouse with Sophie by my side, I was distracted. She seemed unfazed, perfectly ready for everything we faced. She led the way through the establishment's red, double-door entrance, briefly speaking with the hostess.

This wasn't just a casual Japanese restaurant where Americans took what Japanese aspects they wanted to please American customers. The architecture was authentic from the paintings on the walls to the hostess who greeted us at the door and called Sophie's name.

"*Konbanwa*, Sophie-san!" An elderly woman briefly hugged her and spoke softly to her.

Sophie turned to me with a grin. She seemed to have friends everywhere. "Our party hasn't arrived yet, but the room is ready for us."

We left the lobby into the main dining area. Diners ate on small tables on the floor. Servers went from table-to-table, delivering food and taking orders.

The delicious smells wafted from the kitchen and clutched my empty stomach. Back when I was younger, my parents weren't too fond of Japanese food so we hardly ate at any of the restaurants in Phoenix. It was all about home cooked food in the Quinn household.

A young hostess led us past the main dining room to one of the private rooms toward the back. At the entrance to the room, Sophie took off her high heels so I took off my shoes. Once inside, we sat down on cushions next to a table set for six people.

"I thought it was only going to be four of us?" I asked her.

She shrugged. "I don't know who else will be attending."

"Are we too early?"

She winked at me. "We're right on time." She leaned toward me with a conspiratory grin. "Which means the guest of honor is late."

The sliding door opened and Nakamura, along with two other gentlemen, came through a few minutes later. Sophie quickly rose and I repeated her movement. A respectful bow and greeting. Nakamura approached me and I took his hand into both of mine for a firm shake.

So far so good.

Sophie introduced me to Ichiro, Nakamura's first assistant, as well as Takeo, his second assistant.

Nerves aside, I told myself this was the easy part.

We settled into our seats and the conversation was light but went well. My target was all smiles and everything went well, but I couldn't take my mind off the woman next to me. I sat cross-legged on the floor, but her leg was no more than an inch or two from mine. Heat from her side warmed me. She translated whenever it was necessary, but the conversation flowed without problems.

Watching Sophie in action made me proud. While I was all nerves, trying to exude the confidence that rode my back on a daily basis, she seemed to always know the right thing to say. The right conversation started when a topic began to fade away.

Just watching her work made me think of Marcus. Forever the professional. He'd probably work these guys into a buying frenzy.

Sophie's right hand brushed against mine that lay on the floor. She quickly took a drink of water. When her hand came back down, I scooted mine closer until we touched again.

She flashed me a side-glance.

I feigned innocence. I was nothing but an angelic lamb, after all.

Our hostess arrived to let us know our entertainment had arrived. Now that I didn't expect. Two Japanese women entered into the room, both of them dressed in beautiful kimonos. Elaborate pins decorated their finely coiled black hair. They approached us and bowed before the woman who carried an instrument took a place in the corner.

The woman in front us, her lips painted a delicate red, greeted us. "The ladies of the *Ran* troop are pleased to travel from New York to entertain our esteemed guests." Her movements were slow, yet fluid as she began to sing to us. I didn't understand the words, but I couldn't help but be pulled into the tale she told through her music.

While we sipped hot tea drank from tiny cups, I relaxed and enjoyed myself. For once ignoring the man across from me who held the fate of my mission here. By the time the singer was done, I couldn't help but join Sophie in applause.

"She's very talented," I remarked.

Nakamura nodded in agreement.

Once the performance ended and the two women left the room, my nervousness dissipated a bit. Our first course arrived, a serving of hot seafood soup, and I ate every-thing, even if I disliked the taste.

Keep smiling, Xavier.

Over and over again I reminded myself this was the easy part. I waited for Nakamura to ask me questions. I left my eagerness outside of the room and my efforts paid off when he asked about my goals for his facilities. "For the past two years, I've been impressed with research performed by your head researcher, a Dr. Hideo Tanaka. Through our joint efforts, we could increase the 2500T's processor speed by 11%. The profitability margin would be favorable on both ends."

While I continued to speak, Nakamura nodded. When his drink emptied, Sophie, fast as whip, got up to refill his cup. Much faster than Ichiro, I may add. *'Atta girl.*

The drinks and refreshments kept coming. Even as the door opened and an attendant came in to deliver our second course, a large platter of chilean seabass with black bean sauce, I kept going.

I was deep in my flow when suddenly Sophie stopped cold in the middle of pouring a drink for Ichiro. The sliding door to the dining room was still open and her gaze locked on a point outside of the room. For some reason, her face went ashen and she put down the teapot. Without any further words, I watched my assistant get up and bolt from the room.

"Sophie?" I turned to look in the direction she faced, but there was no one there in particular.

THE MOMENT the door closed after her, I rose to get up, but Nakamura extended his hand to stop me.

"Is something wrong with your assistant?" he asked softly.

My whole body stiffened, but I kept my mouth shut instead of making excuses.

Ichiro glanced toward the door. "She didn't even excuse herself. *Women* like that—"

"Just stop right there," I barked to Ichiro. I wanted to knock him on his ass, but I checked myself. "I'm sure Miss Ashton had a good reason for her departure. I don't know you personally, but you shouldn't assume all women behave like that."

"Perhaps she should have—"

I stiffly turned to my host, ignoring Ichiro. "I've enjoyed dinner with you so far, Mr. Nakamura, but I refuse to sit here and let your staff member disrespect mine."

I got up without a second thought, gave Nakamura a deep bow, and left the room.

Contract be damned. Even I had standards.

Chapter Fourteen

Sophie

Sato is here.

But that couldn't be him. He was in Japan.

The moment I stepped out of the room, he was gone. My eyes scanned the noisy dining room, but he wasn't there. Just countless diners—a large family enjoying supper in one corner drew my eye but none of them was him.

Yet, when I hurried down the hall toward the entrance, I saw him again speaking to the hostess and I stopped cold. Sato hadn't changed much. His back was wide and his stance assured. His hair was longer though, cut in a bit in a style that was more Asian than American.

As if pulled by a magnet, I rushed to the door. I had to have my say. He'd have to know how much he hurt me. Sato's name sat at the edge of my tongue, but I never got a chance to speak. He was out the door into the night.

He'd left me again.

A couple walked past me, the man briefly bumping into me. "Excuse me," he said politely.

Reality hit me like a freight train careening off its tracks. *The room. I'd left the dining room.*

Dizziness slammed my senses. I rushed to the bathroom until I hit the cool, tiled wall. From there, I leaned back, letting the cool air from a vent hit my face. My stomach churned painfully. Stirring to the point where I'd purge everything I'd eaten.

Oh fuck, I'd messed up big time. I'd left the room right in front of Nakamura.

I'd left right in front of *my client.*

My insides cringed from such a horrible error. What the hell was I thinking doing that to him?

Damn you, Sophie for choosing your feelings over your work. I'd never done such a thing before and shame filled my face.

Somehow I'd have to walk back into that room and face Xavier. He was most likely furious over what I've done.

Instead of moving though, I waited for my rapidly beating heart to still. For the sweat along my brow to cool. What I'd done flashed through my mind again and again, kicking me in my already aching gut.

You fool, what if you've cost him the contract?

Somehow I forced myself out of the bathroom and I washed my hands. I couldn't setup a new business in the bathroom that was for damn sure. Time to put on my big girl breeches and save face.

I'd prostrate myself on the floor and ask for forgiveness if necessary.

I marched out of the bathroom, confident that I could do this. The moment I reached the private dining room door, my hand hovered over the sliding door handle.

Just open the door.

Yet, I couldn't imagine facing Xavier right now. I didn't have much of a choice though.

Xavier stood there, his mouth set in a hard line. Instead of harsh words, he grabbed my wrist and led me out of the restaurant.

Chapter Fifteen

Xavier

By the time we reached the steps up to the entrance, I released Sophie's arm before I let my growing anger get the best of me. I clenched and unclenched my fists, but I couldn't shake the rising feeling that everything I'd worked for had gone horribly wrong.

I finally turned to her, but she wouldn't look at me though. I waited for the Sophie I knew to speak—to explain what the hell happened—but she didn't.

Above us, the sky was completely dark and clouds were foreboding with the promise of a thunderstorm. Sophie ignored the sight, her arms clasped her sides.

"I deserve an explanation," I finally said.

Her mouth opened, then closed. Frustration shot straight lines across her brow.

I scratched the back of my head and my fingers dug into my scalp to ease the growing tension.

"Dammit, Sophie, I don't know what happened back

there, but you can't just leave like that." I reached for her, but she flinched. "And what did you see——"

"I feel like a fool," she interjected.

I let out a long sigh. I had frustrations of my own and I wanted badly to vent. To tell her she was fired. That she'd never work in the service industry again.

But I didn't.

The growing wind blew her hair toward the west. The tendrils begged me to grasp them. The strong woman who had led me to me this point seemed to have crumbled away and all that was left was the real Sophie.

"This isn't going to work," she said softly.

"Wait a minute. I'm confused." I gestured toward the restaurant. "We messed up big time, but that doesn't mean the fight is over." Sophie might've ended my deal for good, but I'd be damned if I let anyone talk about her that way. Deal or not.

Her face twisted toward me, a wave of anguish washing over her face. "I don't mess up like that. Ever," she snapped. "I was stupid and I made such a dumb mistake when I left."

The words kept tumbling out of her mouth even as the beginning of raindrops hit the tops of our heads. "I didn't think about the contract or you or what you wanted." She swallowed deeply. "It's over. In a minute, you're going to walk away and *anything* that we've agreed to earlier today will mean *nothing.*"

When she finished, she continued to blink from the raindrops.

I took in her beautiful face before I rested my palms on her cheeks. She trembled and I couldn't resist leaning in to kiss her lips. "I'm right here. I haven't gone anywhere. I'm mad, I will admit, but I don't give a fuck about what they think. I walked out of there because I was worried about you, not them."

Uncertainty touched her eyes so I silenced her doubts when I kissed her again. She tasted like sake. A savory, dry taste. My tongue darted out briefly to brush against hers and the moment the tip of our tongues touched I couldn't get enough of her. If I had to, I'd kiss her all night until she didn't have any doubts. No matter how much our clothes became soaked or who passed by. Her hands snaked up my back. My lips trailed up to her chin, tasting the rain before I turned to look at her again.

"Do you remember the offer you kept making me?" she asked.

I nodded.

"I think I'd like those drinks tonight, Mr. Quinn," she whispered.

We didn't say anything to each other as we walked across the street to my apartment, but I kept glancing at her. The way her wet hair clung to her scalp was so sexy. As the elevator road up, I couldn't help looking at the way her nipples poked out of her dress or the way her chest rose and fell. There was no way in fucking hell I wanted those drinks. I wanted Sophie. I wanted her in my bed underneath me and I wanted her crying out my name.

By the time she woke up the next morning she'd have absolutely no doubts that I was the man who wanted her and that I'm the man who wanted to be with her tonight.

Once inside the apartment, the storm really began to pick up and lights flashed outside of the drawn curtains. We stood there in the middle of the living room staring at each other. "Whatever happened to that drink, Mr. Quinn?"

"What would you like to drink?"

"I'd say water," she touched her damp curls, "but I've

had plenty of that so far. How about some of the green tea I left in your fridge."

I slowly smiled. "Where did you find that stuff? It tastes awful."

I shifted to fetch her a drink, but her arms snaked around my waist to hold me close. She pressed her cheek against my shoulder blades and sighed. Her body warmed my back and feelings I thought I'd suppressed since Rosalie passed away rose to the surface. How long ago had I felt longing and inner peace? Years, unfortunately. Tonight wasn't just about me or what I wanted. I placed my hand over hers.

"No drink?" I asked.

She shook her head.

"Your clothes are soaked through, you should take them off."

"And I'm sure you'd like to be the one to take them off." She added space between us I didn't like so I turned to face her.

"I have an IUD," she said. "Have you got condoms?"

I nodded, glad to get that business out of the way.

I moved left as she moved to the right—almost as if we circled each other.

"Take off your shoes," I said.

She did it slowly and I did the same.

"So no pretenses?" she asked.

I shook my head. "We could do some elaborate talk. I could tell you something romantic about what you'd like to do to me, but we both know why we're here. There's some-thing you need and I want to give it to you."

She sucked in a deep breath. "Please...give it to me."

A fire spread through my bones just hearing those bold words from her. Her hands rose to undo a button, but I stopped her by scooping her up in my arms. No more conversation. We needed to use our mouths in other ways. I took two steps at a time up to the second floor. By the time I got to the top, our mouths met again. The kisses were hungry. Feverish. She didn't even give me time to place her on the bed—she ripped my shirt open and tossed what was left to the side. Her blouse got the same treatment as I threw it over the railing and the shirt sailed down to the floor.

Next, I unbuckled her cuffs. Waiting was damn near impossible for me, but I waited to see if she'd protest, but she didn't. I wanted to see her without a stitch of clothing on.

"I can't wait to taste you," I whispered.

Slow down, Xav.

I hungered for her more than should. Over and over again, I tried to slow down as I sampled the skin along her neck, but I couldn't stop myself. I wanted to touch her everyone. Watch every reaction she made.

My tongue swirling along the sensitive points until I encountered her collarbone. Her scent was ever so sweet and delicious, urging me to descend until I encountered her bra. That came off, too.

I made quick work of her panties and soon enough Sophie stood before me. Beautiful, elegant, and sexy. Her pert pink nipples would get my attention soon enough. I lowered my head, taking as much as I could into my mouth. She moaned with each hard suck.

My hands were everywhere, reaching to touch and sample every curve. She was mine tonight. I could take my time and explore every inch of her.

She tried to reach for me to unbutton my belt, but I would have none of that. "Please let me," she begged.

"Don't move an inch." There was no need to rush and I wanted to see her come first. I pushed her back onto the bed and covered her body with mine. Damn, she felt so good. I ran my tongue along the underside of her breast, my nose gently brushing against her. Every shiver she experienced made me want to do more. Like dip my tongue in her navel.

Like dip my tongue in her pussy.

When I parted her thighs, I met no resistance. I trailed kisses along her hipbones, growing hungrier and hungrier as I approached her sex. I hovered over the seam along her lips. Just watching her quiver down there was amazing. It was as if she was a rope, stretched taunt and waiting to be released. Gently I sampled her. A lick here. A teasing suck there. Her thighs clenched around me and she moaned. When she got close, I pulled back.

"Please, Xavier," she begged.

She'd come soon enough, but she wasn't ready yet.

I inserted two fingers into her wet channel. Her pussy pulsated against my fingers. Her back arched and she cried out my name.

With one hand on her stomach and the other holding her legs open so that I could taste her, I could feel the trembling of her stomach muscles. The contracting and clenching, in time with the soft moans from between her lips. She was getting close again, practically ready to come, but then she reached for me.

"Xavier…"

I pulled her hands away. "I told you not to move."

I got up. From my drawer I pulled out two silk ties. Nice from enough to do the job I wanted.

"Up against the headboard," I said.

She quickly complied, scooting upwards while she watched me. She seemed so small near such a huge bedpost. From the first day I met her, I imagined seeing her like this.

Gently, I tied each of her wrists to the headboard.

"Does it hurt, sweetheart?" I asked.

She shook her head. "No…"

I had to take a step back to see how beautiful she was. With the added distance between us, I could see the feverish pitch in her eyes. The tension in her limbs as if she reached for me. She waited to be possessed.

You could have like this forever if you opened up and let her love you.

But I didn't need forever. Life wasn't a guarantee thing, and yet, as I approached her again, I could shake the need want forever with Sophie.

She kept perfectly still with each step I took to the bed. Her gaze never wavered. Silence in the room stretched out as I crept along her body, feeling her twitch when our bodies came in contact. I couldn't resist smiling at her while my nose drifted over her clit.

"Please…"

If I pressed her here, she'd come. "Please what? What do you want me to do to you, Sophie?"

She squirmed, her hips bucking toward my hand.

"Tell me," I asked again.

"I need you. I want you."

"And who is going to make you come?"

"You will."

I discarded the rest of my clothes. The condom went on next.

She waited patiently without words.

So I gave her what she needed and caressed the soft skin below her breasts to the firm muscles on her slim legs. She shuddered beneath me and the ties flexed as she pulled at them to reach for me. All the while, I watched her face and enjoyed the way her legs wrapped around my hips as if she never wanted me to leave.

I watched her face while I slid into her warmth, taking in the molten heat of her eyes and passionate way her fingernails bit into my shoulder blades. This was where I truly wanted to be, over her, inside her, feeling her heart race as quickly as mine.

~

Sophie

Never would I have imagined myself being tied up in Xavier's bed.

And yet, now that he was inside of me, I didn't want this feeling to end. The tension in my clit spread everywhere. Much faster than I was ready for it. Tighter and tighter. The delicious stretch along my rib cage up to my arms only intensified.

My climax came fast and hard.

But he kept going, filling me again and again. All I could do to hold onto him was wrap my legs around his hips and accept what he gave me.

Delicious pleasure coursed up my spine, drenching me with his sweat as he filled my body again and again. He nibbled my neck while I tasted the salty sweat on his skin.

When he came, I clung to him, my fingernails digging into his back.

Using his elbows, he propped himself up, but his forehead continue to rest in the crook of my neck. His harsh cries of pleasure warmed my skin and I loved feeling the heaviness of his body on mine. Moments like this I wanted to reach out and run my fingers through his hair, but with my arms bound all I could do was imagine it.

Soon enough though he reached for my wrists and

untied me. The delicious burn in the muscles along my arms felt good.

"You all right?" he asked me.

"I think you know the answer to that question." I was probably smiling like a fool.

He chuckled and briefly his head lowered to kiss my nose. My face was warm. Even after what happened he knew how to make me feel special. "I don't know why I waited so long to do this to you."

I knew very well why it took us so long to do this. We both had doubts, and just like him, this was new territory for me. With Sato everything had been private from the get go. With Xavier there were no boundaries.

"What are you thinking about?" he asked.

"So did you actually have plans to give me that drink?"

With the devilish grin he left the bed. I watched his ass as he made his way down the stairs. I stretched out under the covers, languishing and enjoying this moment. I only had a second to briefly close my eyes before I heard him coming back up the steps. Even with the dim light from a lamp downstairs, I could make out his beautiful form. His walk was so graceful, so self-assured. Without a stitch of clothing on I could make out every single muscle. Xavier Quinn was a beautiful specimen.

But as he got closer to the bed I noticed something in particular. There was a scar along his kneecap. On such a perfect body it wasn't hard to miss such a thing. What had happen to him? Was he in an accident of some kind? As he got closer, I couldn't see any other scars and the line was perfectly straight. Almost is it cut from surgery? Had something happened to his knee a long time ago?

I took the bottle of water he offered with a smile. "What happened to you?"

I reached out and brushed my fingertips against his knee.

He shrugged. "It's nothing." He turned away as if that would be the only answer I'd get. I tried to broach the subject further, but he ran his hands from my arm over the curve of my hip and down my leg.

"There's so many other things we could be doing," he remarked. "I'd rather be looking at you. I'd rather be inside you."

I couldn't stop smiling. "I can't think of a reason to tell you no..."

～

Sophie

The morning after amazing sex was the best. There was nothing better than waking up with someone beside you. You're sore. You're exhausted. But you didn't care because the one who made you that way was next to you. That was how I felt when I woke up next Xavier. I wrapped my arms around him and ran my nose across his hard pecs.

I could do this every hour of the day if it were possible. His skin was so smooth and if I put my nose in just the right place and I drew in a deep breath, I caught a lingering smell of his cologne.

All the while, he seemed to quietly sleep and let me stare at him.

Then a flicker of fear touched my stomach.

Don't get too attached to him. Don't fall in love with him, Sophie.

But repeating that to myself over and over again didn't work. This felt so right laying next to him, enjoying having his body next to mine. I'd been alone for so damn long and

I practically wanted to bottle this moment so that I could sample it at night after he left.

A thought came to mind that I could leave the bed right now and just walk away. Once I talked to him later, there'd be no messy breakups. No awkward moments between us. Just two adults making the decision to part ways, but a lot of things were easier said than done.

Eventually, I settled back into his arms and drifted back to sleep again. After countless nights of getting no more than three to four hours of sleep, somehow I slept until noon.

It was bliss.

By the time I did get up to shower, my muscles protested every move, but the pain was good and I welcomed it. Xavier didn't wake when I left. He just rolled over in his sleep and murmured softly. I reached over and ran my fingers through his hair. Even if things ended between us today, I still had enough memories to last me for a long time to come.

Chapter Sixteen

Xavier

Sophie was in the shower by the time I got up. Damn, I thought I practically lived in the shower, but she had me beat. Just thinking about her standing in the water running a bar of soap over her perfect tits made my dick hard in anticipation for round two. Or was that round five? *Ehh, who's counting?*

She probably hadn't been in there for too long. I could probably still help soap her down before she gets out...

I leaned out of the bed and noticed something on the end table. The leather cuffs I'd taken off of Sophie's wrists sat next to my wristwatch. I picked one of them up. I've never really seen them up close before.

They seemed so simple. A bit worn, but the leather was still tough. Why did she like these so much? I'd never tied up a woman using something like this before so I only had a vague idea about why she liked them. On the closer examination, I spotted small letters branded on the inside. They seemed so tiny. Far too tiny to be the brand name.

The leather wasn't cheap and the craftsmanship was fine, but when I looked on the outside I didn't see any manufacturer labels.

Now that I thought about it, these weren't letters, but Asian symbols. Maybe Chinese or Japanese. Naturally, I had no idea what they meant, yet both of the symbols were on the left and the right wrist cuffs. Was that the name of the manufacturer? Or someone's name? The idea that Sophie wore something with another man's name made me uncomfortable, but I didn't know what they meant so I returned the wrist cuffs to where I'd found them.

I finally got up to join her in the shower, but she came out of the bathroom with a towel wrapped around herself.

She made a face, apparently catching me in the act. "What are you doing with those?"

"They look pretty cool. I've never seen you *not* wearing them before."

She picked them up, but that wouldn't end my curiosity. "There was something carved into the leather. Is that Japanese?"

She feigned disinterest. "It's nothing."

I paused for moment, staring her down and she stared right back at me. "That's it?"

The slight curve of the side of lip was mesmerizing. "Yep."

~

Sophie

By the time Xavier had finished his shower, I'd already prepared a spinach omelet for him with some coffee.

When I darted my head into his bathroom to tell him such, I almost had to dart back out.

Steam had filled the room and the mirrors were fogged up. Xavier stood under the shower with his eyes shut. I could only make out his profile through the glass. From his long legs to the curve of his perfect ass. He turned briefly to reveal his wide back. Warmth touched my cheeks and my stomach quivered, remembering what he did to me last night. The temptation to discard my clothes and joined him seemed like a good idea, but I remained where I stood.

Don't get too close. That doesn't belong to you, Sophie. You lived in the moment and got what you needed. Time to go.

I sucked in a deep breath and took in the scent of his soap. Enticing and spicy. All male.

So am I borrowing him for a little while? I asked myself. Seemed like a simple enough question and rationalizing the situation like he was a bicycle or a cup of sugar made me giggle.

'Cause if he was a bike, he offered a nice, hard ride.

"I'm leaving now," I managed to call out. "I made you some breakfast."

The door to the shower opened and he peered around it. Water dripped down his forehead and my eyes followed the trail down his chest. When my gaze came back up, the dark look in his eyes told me I'd been caught staring him down.

"So soon?" He ran his tongue along his bottom lip. I wanted to be that lip.

Somehow, I found the ability to form coherent words. "Yeah, I need to clear out my schedule." *So that absolutely nothing will keep me from seeing you again if you need me.*

He nodded. "There's plenty of room in here."

This was the part where I was supposed to close the door, but I didn't. Drinking him in seemed far more appealing.

"Come here." He beckoned me with his outstretched hand, but I still had a bit of resolve left.

Before I had a chance to think about it further, Xavier left the shower, strode across the room, and scooped me up in his arms.

Again.

Our mouths met by the time he was halfway across the room and I couldn't speak. Couldn't protest. Who the hell would protest when a naked man, practically good enough to eat, swept you off your feet and took you into a shower?

He placed me on my feet on the tiled floor. Only to back me to the wall hard enough to take my breath away. Rational thought should've intruded when he ripped my blouse open and then unzipped the back of my skirt. My clothes fell to the wet floor. His caresses left me heady, hungry for more than his mouth.

With a jerk, he turned me around. The wall tiles against my face were wet and warm. His body pressed against mine, the scorching heat of his erection searing my ass. He made quick work of unsnapping my bra and discarding my skirt. All the while, his pace quickened.

"So beautiful," he whispered as his hands descended down my back. Not quickly, but slowly and sensually.

His fingers trailed down the seam of my bottom, eliciting a quake within me. Warm lips kissed my shoulder blades and my heart swelled each time he brushed against me.

Was this what letting go felt like? This weightless feeling that made me eager to be with him again and again.

Xavier's hands circled my hips and he pulled me back against his hard chest. Ever so slowly, he slid inside of me, gliding into my channel with three fingers. The exquisite touch left me wanting more. Somehow, I managed to turn around to kiss him again. His hungry mouth devoured mine. I reached down between us, running my hands over his hard pecs, even lower until I grasped his length.

He hissed against my lips. *Now that's what I wanted to hear.*

Our gazes locked while he thrust his fingers into me as I stroked his length. He stared me down, almost challenging me to come first.

I'm not tied down today, Mr. Quinn.

Using the soap, I gripped the base with one hand and stroked upwards. As my pleasure built from his attention, my grip faltered a few times.

"Is that all you got?" he grunted.

I stroked him faster.

My breasts bounced with each of his thrusts. Pleasurable agony pooled in my stomach and raced down my legs. His thumb on my clit was blissful punishment that kept increasing in intensity.

"Xavier…" his name slipped out of my mouth, followed by a long moan. He had me right where he wanted me, pinned where I couldn't escape my oncoming orgasm.

Until he paused.

"What's—" I began.

"Are you going to run away next time when I ask you to stay?" His hard gaze bore into me and the icy steel in his voice was unmistakable.

Did he seriously ask me a question right before I was ready to come? I ran my thumb across the tip of his cock. He flinched, but he still didn't move.

"*Answer me, Sophie.*" His eyebrows lowered and his mouth formed a hard line.

"No," I murmured, so close to climax the muscles in my legs began to go out.

"When I tell you to come to me, you will," he whispered against my mouth. He thrust harder into me. Faster. My back arched in response. My breath came out in punctuated gasps. Pretty soon I was bucking against him, practically writhing until he pushed me over the edge and I cried out.

When my breaths evened out, all I could hear was the hiss of the shower. The smell of sex lingered in the air, but I just stood there like a dazed fool while Xavier gave me a pleased smile.

He picked up the soap and slowly cleansed my body. By the time he was done, I had most of my faculties back, along with the awareness of one thing: I didn't want to run away as much anymore.

Not if this was the happy ending I'd always get.

Chapter Seventeen

Sophie

After my unsuccessful escape from Xavier's place, I was much more self-conscious about being around him. Once I got back to my apartment around lunchtime, I was surrounded and interrogated like any good friend should be.

"Don't you have a job?" I asked Penny.

"Not right now. You're not that slick, sweetie. How long were you going to wait before you told us what's going on between you and the *Xavier Quinn*?" she asked. I'd found her camped out on the couch with sleepy eyes, a relaxed smile, and messy hair. She'd been out all night, most likely at the Phoenix Club, a local BSDM club. "Dinner is one thing, but you've been seeing him often."

The door to Lana's bedroom was closed for once.

"What are you doing on the couch?" I asked. "Did you pull an all-nighter?"

She looked me over with pursed lips. "Oh, you're not

avoiding my question that easily. You left yesterday with different clothes on and never came home."

I picked up a few containers of Thai food someone had left on the coffee table. A great distraction. She'd follow me to my room anyway. "I had a dinner meeting and such with Mr. Quinn."

"And?" she pressed.

I tossed the food in the trash. There was no way I was letting one of my roommates eat them as leftovers. "And we had additional work to do."

"I bet they *worked* all right," a voice behind me said.

I turned around to see Lana, dressed only in a long Harvard U T-shirt, along with a shirtless man in jeans trailing after her. We had a guest. Now that was a new development.

"Morning!" the man said as I began to prepare coffee. He had that scruffy look to him. Definitely not my type, but he was cute nonetheless.

Lana mimed pushed the two digits of her right hand into her cupped left. A rather crass gesture, if you asked me. And anyway, he didn't use two fingers. He used three.

"Oh, stop it," I said with a laugh. "Who's your friend?"

"She's stalling, don't fall for it," Penny said.

Lana introduced me to Dr. Hanley. The name seemed vaguely familiar.

"Tongue-surf guy?" I mouthed to Penny.

She nodded back with a devilish grin. I guess Lana's vow of celibacy was officially over.

Lana ran her hand down our guest's wide—yet slightly hairy back—and turned back to me. "So are you two dating or what?" she asked me.

If she would've gotten to the point any faster I might've experienced whiplash. "Not exactly. It's complicated."

Weren't all relationships?

"So did you have wild, hot monkey sex last night?" Penny's face brightened.

"For someone who didn't sleep in their own bed last night, you sure have a lot of questions," I replied to her.

She went to the coffee maker with a grin. "Best couch nap ever." The rich smell of coffee filled the kitchen as she poured herself a cup from the large carafe. "Sophie, this is the first time I've seen you stay out overnight with someone. I just wanted to make sure you're happy."

"I'm good." Satisfied. Fulfilled. Any similar words would be appropriate. Carlie would say *well-fucked*, but that wasn't my style though.

"Carlie told me he's a celebrity. We just want you to be careful," Penny added. "He might be here one minute and gone the next. Not the best marriage material."

I almost replied, "Just the way I want it," but I didn't feel like saying it. I nodded instead.

Now that the interrogation ended, I managed to snag some coffee and run away to my room. Once there I checked my message service. Soon enough I could be buried in my work and any distractions related to Xavier Quinn could be cast away.

Only to find any empty inbox.

I wasn't surprised about this development either. I got a huge ass check from one of the richest people in the world and my assistant eagerly accepted the additional hours.

At the rate Jesse was going, I could leave my business behind and join Carlie.

For the first time in a long time, I spent the day doing things I rarely had an opportunity to accomplish: Clearing out old documents for shredding, dusting my room, you know, boring crap most folks forget about until they were stuck at home.

Now that I was organizing my space, I also went

through all the white boxes from Sato. It was time to get rid of them. Instead of throwing them in the trash, I decided I'd just take out the gift and toss out the boxes.

Sounds easy enough right?

I formed a pile in the middle of the room. The newer packages on the bottom with the older ones on top.

Armed with a box cutter, I got to work on the first one. With each rip, I steeled myself for what I'd find. In the first one, I pulled out a letter and a necklace. I crumbled up the letter and tossed the paper into the waste bin. *Oh, look, three points!*

By the fourth box, I was on a roll, until I read the letter inside. The letter had come at a time when I'd been at my lowest point, depressed and hardly eating:

Sophie,

Each time I write these letters, I pretend you're not mad at me and you're happy. Pretending won't change things though. Are you well today? I just became district manager for my father's company. My parents held a party for me and I thought of you the entire time.

My heartbeat still speeds up every time I think of our first night together. During the other times my heart hurts to think about the ocean that separates us. Please understand that I had no choice. As the heir to my family, I must choice them first.

Sato

A growing anger made me clench the letter tight enough crumble it a bit. *He thought of me the entire time?* I guess when he got on the plane to leave me behind I slipped his mind.

And I absolutely detested myself for feeling a brief moment of happiness when he mentioned how he fondly thought of our first time together. That had been a special moment for me and he'd *ruined* it in this letter. *That bastard.*

Instead of tossing the note in the trash, I grabbed the next box. I'd been stabbed in the gut, I might as well go for jugular. Box after box held letter after letter. Not one of them apologized to me. In each of them, he expressed how much he missed me and how he wanted to be with me again if he ever came back to the US.

I tore open the latest one and dared myself to read it. My hands shook as I wiped away the tears that fell.

Sophie,

I'm coming to the US and I want to see you.

Sato

So I had seen him at Sakura No Hana. It didn't matter though. Sato still knew how to hurt me without saying a word.

BY THE NEXT DAY, I was ready to escape. I had yet to get any texts from Xavier about Nakamura and I grew worried. Had what happened at the teahouse messed up any chances he had for a contract?

An ache grew in my chest. Xavier might've tried to sooth my ruffled feathers but the truth of the matter was that people like him had far loftier goals than my concierge business in Boston. He employed thousands of people. What if my actions kept him from doing something far greater than I could imagine? I wasn't a fool. I'd done my research. Xavier had big plans on pushing mobile technology from the research level into the practical form. Every single day I saw someone holding a cellphone. I used one all the time, but I never thought about the people behind the technology. It took capital and drive to innovate and Xavier had both of those.

I had no idea what he'd told Nakamura the other day, but I did understand that billions of people used phones, and mobile devices required a processor to function. A faster processor meant cellphones could do more and Xavier needed Nakamura to accomplish this goal.

And I was one of the critical people for this mission. *No pressure, huh?*

Maybe I'd heard what I wanted to hear two days ago about how everything was all right and now his silence was a loud and clear message: *you messed up.*

Rain continued to fall, so I worked alone in my room until my phone bleeped with a new message: *Come to the Andretti Cigar Club. Private smoking room 4. Men's T-shirt and panties only. Wait for me.*

My jaw dropped. What kind of request was this? Instead of revulsion, my heart sped up.

Wasn't this what I wanted? To see him again?

When I call for you, you'll come to me. That was what he'd said.

There was no hesitation in my step when I dressed in a thong and garters. I put on my trench coat over my naked-ness. The men's T-shirt could be bought on the way.

No one questioned me when I left the apartment in black heels. It was just another day, another dime for their roommate who catered to the rich.

I took a cab from my place to downtown. The traffic was heavy into the city due to an accident on the express-way, but once I was past the slow crawl, the cab's speed picked up. I kept glancing at my watch. Xavier really hadn't specified a time.

Would he show up and not find me there?

By the time my cab pulled up next to the cigar bar, the traffic was thick along 9th Street. I glanced at my phone. Did I have enough time to get a shirt? I'd rather show up properly than not all so I hurried to the closet shop and bought a shirt.

When I returned to the cigar bar, I was relieved to

learn from the hostess that the party for the private room had yet to arrive. As I weaved through the main bar with its brick walls, leather seats and modern decor, I was pleased at the chance to come to this place. Not a single client in the past had asked for accommodations here.

Every kind of cigar connoisseur drank and smoked here. From the guy we passed in jeans and polo to a woman dressed in what had to be the sharpest Chanel pantsuit I'd ever seen. A light fog of cigar smoke filled the air, ranging from roasted nuts, leather, even coffee.

I was led to an elevator that took me to the second floor with the private party rooms. One door was open already with a lively party going on inside. I spied only men enjoying cocktails and cigars. Maybe a bachelor's party.

My private room was gorgeous. At the other end of the room, from the cedar wood floors to the ceiling, windows offered a view of downtown. Along the other wall was a private bar and selection of cigars. The room had every-thing from cutters to lighters. I didn't dare touch anything. The cost alone to book this room and have everything available had to be in the thousands.

Then I spied a tiny box in the center of one of the black leather seats. The box had a tiny label: SIT HERE.

Inside the box was a piece of chocolate. I popped the piece into my mouth and discovered the center was filled with candied vodka. *Very nice and smooth.*

Time to get ready. I took off my coat and donned the shirt. It practically covered nothing more than my ass. There went picking the right size. At least I was warm. The room was cooler than I preferred.

I sat down where he wanted me, turned away from the door. Was this what he did with all the women he dated?

Waiting like this used to be easy. Not so much anymore.

The large hand on the clock continued to tick, tick, tock and for some reason I kept glancing at it.

He's coming, Sophie. He's not Sato.

The room was stony quiet. Except for the sounds next door. Would any of the guys who cat-called in my direction come inside? *Not the best way to keep your shiny, clean image, Ashton!*

But it was too late now.

My heartbeat raced in anticipation. Memories from the encounter at the park flooded my mind and my thighs clenched with need. The large shirt hid the pebbling of my breasts.

The door opened with an audible yawn. The urge to turn around was strong, but I ignored it and faced forward.

Before Sato I had little patience, but one thing I quickly learned was that rewards came to those who waited. Pleasure came with obedience.

I licked my dry lips and kept my gaze fixed on the window.

Xavier strolled past me and took a seat across from me. He smelled absolutely delicious and looked gorgeous in his dark blue suit.

"Sorry to keep you waiting so long."

"It's not long at all." I would've waited longer. Especially for the self-assured man in front of me.

His gaze swept over me from my heels, up my legs and finally to the shirt I wore. I squirmed under his scrutiny. Was he already as hungry for his touch as he was for mine.

"Why haven't you contacted me?" I finally asked.

"I've been rather busy with affairs back west."

"So everything is going well with Nakamura?"

He nodded. "As expected."

I tried to keep a straight back, but all the uncertainties that flicked at me earlier made it hard for me to keep my cool. I had so many questions to ask him and none of them seemed to want to come out of my mouth. Had he thought of me since I'd left his apartment? Had what occurred between us meant anything to him other than casual sex?

"Please elaborate," was all I said.

"He's taken an interest in me beyond our meeting. That much I'm sure of. My associates at Silver Sparrow told me someone from Nakamura's company is examining my holdings." Every word he spoke, I couldn't keep my eyes off his mouth. Those lips that sucked on me in the shower. Those large hands that had made me come in the shower.

I tried to smile and couldn't stop my legs from crossing and uncrossing. I had to be sopping wet against the seat. "That's a good sign. We're getting close."

He watched me for a moment and I would have given everything I had to know what he was thinking. What was going through his mind? Half of the time I thought I understood my clients. Their needs and their desires. That was my job, but at this moment I wasn't sure how to please.

What I did know was that I *wanted* to please him. To serve him.

My mouth opened, but no sound came out.

"Open your shirt, please," he finally said.

My fingers trembled, yet I managed to begin unbuttoning the shirt. From the top, down to the bottom, my skin was exposed to the cool air in the room. By the time I was done, my chest rose and fell in time with my rapid heartbeat. I pulled the shirt open, exposing my breasts to him. The nipples were pert and ready to be sucked. When I looked up, he was staring at me.

"I'd like a bourbon please," he added.

"Of course." I rose from the seat and went to the private bar. Everything had been stocked from the hard liquors to the martini mixes. Nothing but the best. I selected a personal favorite from the bourbons and poured him a shot with two ice cubes. Once done, I strolled over to him and placed the drink on the table beside him. Instead of looking at his face, I couldn't tear my gaze away from the hand that rested on his leg. His hand was a hairs breath away from my knee. Close enough to caress me if he saw fit.

He wasn't done ordering me around. "A Cuban, please."

Another thrill coursed through me. I fetched a cigar from the selection, as well as a cutter and a lighter. I didn't smoke, but I knew how to handle them. I was a quick learner after a client requested a box from overseas. With ease I cut the end off then I approached him again, putting the cigar in his opened mouth. The way his lips wrapped around the cigar made my mouth water, almost if he drew my breast between his lips.

Using the lighter, I drew a flame over the end as he puffed. When he exhaled, the smell of citrus and wood filled the room.

Damn, he even made smoking a cigar sexy as hell.

"Take off your panties and give them to me."

I did as he requested.

"Go back to the chair and sit," he said.

He took a sip of his bourbon before he spoke again. A faint haze from the smoke surrounded him, adding to delicious smell of his cologne.

"Sit back in the chair and open your legs."

I hesitated, but did as I was told. What did he want me to do this time?

"Run your fingers down between your breasts..."

My gaze locked with his, I ran my fingertips along my

collarbone down to my sternum. Goosebumps formed along the path.

"Down farther," he whispered, drawing in a single puff of his cigar. "All the way to your cunt."

When my fingertips brushed against my mound, I sucked in a breath. I'd played this game before, but I'd been alone before. Not like this in a well-lit room with a man like Xavier Quinn watching my every move.

"Open yourself to me. Show me how wet you are." His voice was husky now, desiring lining his words.

I did as he told me to do. It was easy to imagine it was his hands on me.

"Rub your clit for me. That's it."

As my pleasure began to grow, I had to close my eyes. One moment I was sitting there watching him watch me, and in the next, I imagined him perched in front of me, one of his hands holding one of my thighs up on my armrest, while another one was between my legs using all his fingers to rub my clit. My lower lips trembled. I kept going. He was right there with me, drawing me in, pulling me to moment I wanted to reach, but never could. A peak that only another man had helped me climb.

"Open your eyes, Sophie," Xavier bit out.

Through slit eyes, I looked at him. I was so close. I already had two fingers inside of my channel and my pace was frenzied.

"Look at me," he said again. "You came here when I told you to do so, but will you *come* when I command it?"

"Yes," I murmured.

"Stop."

I did as I was told, but my sex continued to clench around my hand.

"I like watching your face when you're like this," he said. "So close. So ready."

Yes, he did love to watch. He loved to observe. He loved to control. Just like Sato but in a different way.

I trembled against my hand.

"I want to see you come now, Sophie."

With a flick of my wrist I began again and it only took a few strokes for me to climax. For my whole body to shudder and for my senses to spark like lightning from a bright thunderstorm.

Sated, I rested the back of my head against the seat.

"Would you like something to drink?" he was standing above me with a napkin to wipe off my hands.

"Thanks," I murmured.

After I cleaned off my hands, I found it hard to look at him while he worked at the tiny bar. So I focused on the drink he offered me: an Irish Cream Coffee.

"Good choice," I said after a sip. "You're a good bartender."

He leaned down, scooped me up, and sat back down with me in his lap. The gesture was so unexpected I froze in place. The cup hovered near my lips, but I didn't so much as drink while I rested against him.

The moment was too perfect to ruin.

Maybe if I took a drink or if I snuggled further against his chest, he'd stop slowly stroking my legs. If I spoke I might break the spell and he'd stop resting his lips against my forehead.

Instead of moving, I closed my eyes and breathed in his cologne. I couldn't get enough of it.

Time passed. I wasn't sure how long, but the cup I held wasn't warm anymore.

"Sophie," he finally murmured against my skin.

"Yes?" I whispered.

I waited for his reply, but the words never came. When

I couldn't wait any longer, I turned to look at him. "You okay?"

Instead of a relaxed look on his face, a pensive Xavier Quinn stared back at me. "Tell me more about yourself?"

I swallowed deeply. Didn't a man like him with every resource imaginable know all my secrets?

"What do you want to know?"

"The basics. Are you from Boston?" *So he hadn't looked me up...*

"Not originally. I was born in NYC." I relaxed against him and told him about how I grew up with Carlie, Penny, and Griff. Thinking of them made me smile. "We used to get into trouble together all the time. Back when we were maybe eight or nine, we used to cross this lady's backyard to avoid gang members who blocked a corner off 145th Street. Two of the planks in her fence was loose so we'd shift them just enough to squeeze inside." I closed my eyes as the memories flooded me. "One day we saw a pie left out to cool off on a table. Of course, being hungry kids, Carlie took the lead and made off with the pie. Her partner-in-thievery, Penny, trailed after her. And, oh man, that pie was so good."

It was the small memories like these reminded me of how lucky I was having close friends. "A few days later, we found more food outside. Baloney and cheese sandwiches. Cake on rare occasions. I guess she took pity on a bunch dirty kids no one wanted." I swallowed from remembering something I'd buried. "I never learned her name, but one day the fence was fixed and that was the end of our adventures. I guess she'd died."

I lay against him, happy to have shared something only my closest friends knew. Carlie would probably be mortified to know I shared such a thing. We sat quietly for a while until he spoke.

"I have business to attend to this afternoon. Stay in the room as long as you like." He stood and placed me back into the seat. "Chris can drive you home when you're ready."

I opened my mouth to ask him to stay, but the terms of our arrangement flashed before my eyes. We were seeing where this went, but this wasn't permanent. At that moment, I realized *all I do is wait*. Maybe I waiting for Xavier to say he was going to stay instead of leave. My fists clenched as my heart lurched.

This is for the best, Sophie, I told myself. *You don't need to get hurt again.*

So why did it hurt to see him leave?

Chapter Eighteen

Xavier

The minute I walked out of the Andretti Cigar Bar, I regretted leaving so soon, but it had to be done.

Every step I took away from the bar was sure. For the last few days, I couldn't stop thinking about her. Focusing on my work or the contract had become near impossible. All I could do was think about reasons so that we could be together.

I couldn't think of anything without outright telling her I wanted to be with her.

So I sent her a text to go to the cigar club and now I was walking away without telling how I really felt.

Frustrated, I ran my fingers through my hair. I'd lied to her for a second time when I told her I business to attend to. I did—in a way—but I owned my company for goodness sake. If I wanted to postpone a meeting for a few hours I could do that.

But I didn't have the balls to tell her that I was falling

for her. Over and over again I told myself this was all about the mission at hand. Secure the contract and go back home.

My phone rang in my pocket. Probably Sophie ready to curse my name. I was surprised to see it was Marcus.

"What's up?" I said after I heard him call my name.

"You're probably gonna be pissed at me, but I'm actually here in Boston."

"Really?" I stopped short in middle of the sidewalk, managing to avoid some puddles.

"I'm here with Becca for a few days and I wanted to eat dinner with you tonight? Could you manage to fit us in?" His voice seemed strained. What the hell was going on?

"Of course. I'll have my assistant make the arrangements." I paused. My brother and I had never had such conversations for the last couple of years. As Mr. Dependable, he never needed anything from me and I thought the same from him.

With a single phone call Marcus had an uncanny way of making things happen. Need a last minute distributor for furniture—one showed up in an hour. Need a last minute caterer? Marcus had that on speed-dial, too.

Maybe that was why my parents chose him to take over the Quinn family business—the management of a chain of luxury resorts in the Southwest. I was the college dropout who didn't even have a finance degree to his name. For the past couple of years, as I watched Marcus, with his own growing family, get closer to my parents, I kept telling myself things turned out for the better. My company's profit margin was much higher. My older brother, who I still admired, got all the glory.

It was the best for everyone, right?

"How does eight sound for dinner then?" I asked.

"That sounds great. We'll see you then."

Sophie

I wasn't sure how long I sat in the private room at the cigar club, but it was long enough for me to count the number of whiskey bottles along the wall. When I got to forty, I got dressed and went home.

As I walked into my apartment I wished Xavier were standing here so I could argue with him. Maybe throw a "who do you think you are?" or two at him. He couldn't just spend time with me and walk out after all the things he said about seeing where things went.

We've agreed to see where this takes us, was what he'd said. *Entanglements or not.*

As I took off my heels in the living room I spied Penny reading a magazine at the tiny kitchen table.

"Where's Lana?" I asked.

Penny bit her lower lip and shrugged. "She's in her room and she hasn't come out since she got back from campus. I think it's over with Doctor McDreamy."

"Why?" He didn't look half bad. Except the hairy back.

"One of her busybody classmates found out about them and told the Dean. Lana was called in and I'm sure you can guess what happened after that."

I groaned. "Poor thing. Maybe I should make her some tea."

"I already offered her candy, tea, and even an app on my phone where she could beat up a doll that had a picture of the Dean's face on it. She just wanted some time alone."

My phone vibrated in my purse. If it was Xavier, I wasn't interested in doing any work for him.

"Then I'll wait for her to come out. We should order a pizza tonight and watch something classic to brighten our moods."

"*You've Got Mail*," Penny tossed in.

"I was thinking more along the lines of *Roman Holliday*."

"Unrequited love. How about *Notting Hill*?"

We could do this for days. My phone rang again. "I have to see who's calling, but after I order the pizza later, we're going to watch *My Fair Lady*."

"After we watch *Say Anything...*"

Once I reached the privacy of my room, I answered the phone. It wasn't Xavier.

"Sophie-san, I hope you don't mind this phone call," Komiko began, "but I felt the need to reach out to you."

Now this was unexpected. I greeted Komiko, even bowing a bit while holding the phone. "I don't mind at all. How did you find my number?"

"I called your business and a lovely gentleman forwarded me to you."

Good 'ole Jesse.

"I see. What can I do for you?" I asked.

"It's something I'd like to do for you."

I sat on the edge of my bed. What could I need from her?

"Sato is getting married in a few months."

A tsunami crushed me, but I didn't miss a beat with a quick reply. "Please congratulate him for me."

"He is here in Boston, Sophie-san," she said simply.

She was silent for a bit, maybe to let that information sink in. "The way you two parted has not sat well with me. I've spoken to Sato about it and scolded him like a good auntie." That made me smile a bit. "You were so sweet and had such a kind soul. When he told me not to contact you again two years ago, I suspected you had ended things, but later I learned from him that he was the one who cut off all ties with you."

Hearing all this sucked the air out of my lungs. I wish she were in front of me right now so that I could hug her —even though she wasn't much of the hugging type.

"I think it's time for you and Sato to meet. He needs to do the honorable thing and explain himself to you. I'll contact you soon to make the arrangements."

By the time I wrapped up my phone call with Komiko, my heart was still beating so fast, I placed my palm to my chest to feel to rapid thumps. I sucked in a deep breath or two, willing myself to calm down.

Why was I feeling nervous about a man I'd forgotten about?

Because you need to see him one more time, I reminded myself. For closure.

Then my phone vibrated with a new message.

Xavier

The afternoon went by faster than I'd expected. I sent a request, as well as an apology to Sophie. She called me back and we spoke briefly. She said she'd make the arrangements for dinner with my brother.

"I expect you to be there, Miss Ashton."

"Of course." Her reply was pensive, but she didn't speak any further on the matter.

Not long before Chris took me to pick up Sophie, I got another phone call I'd been waiting for from one of my associates at Silver Sparrow.

"Sorry for the delay, Mr. Quinn. Our branch office manager in Shanghai got back to us on the symbols on the photo you emailed us."

"And what do they mean?" I asked her.

"It's not a what, Mr. Quinn, it's a who. Haruto Sato is the name of the son of one of the most prominent banking firms in Nagasaki. According to the information I obtained, he went to school at Tokyo University and then did his graduate studies in NYC. After that, he began an internship at a firm in Boston."

Now she really had my attention. "During what time period?"

The sounds of papers moving. "Two years ago. After that he relocated back to Japan and now he works for his family's company."

"I see."

Jealousy circled in my stomach, clinging to me in a way I didn't like. So all this time she wore something from another man. A man who didn't even live in the United States anymore.

"Thank you for your diligent work." I said my good-byes and ended the call. Naturally, my head swam with the information I'd acquired.

Were they still together? I shook my head. Sophie wasn't the kind of person to do that kind of thing, and yet, as I looked at the brief email on who Sato was, I couldn't shake the feeling that kept surging. I wanted to storm over to her place and rip those cuffs off her arms.

I picked up my phone, but stopped.

What the hell are you doing, Xav?

You have to be delusional to think you're falling for this woman. You're crossing a line you told yourself you wouldn't cross. Even if someone else has branded her as his, you can't have her that way.

I always had a reason for doing what I did. That was my way. So what reason did have to care about Haruto Sato?

When I couldn't think of a reason not to finish my phone call, I went ahead and dialed the number I needed.

To hell with lines. A barrier never stopped me in the past.

I ARRIVED at Sophie's house a bit before seven-thirty. To my delight she wasn't ready. Catching her off guard was becoming one of the highlights of my day.

Lana answered the door, pizza in hand with a grin. Compared to the other times I'd seen her, she appeared a bit more out of it today. Her *Green Day* T-shirt swallowed her body.

"I was hoping to see you again," the redhead said. "I didn't know if you'd left town yet."

"My business isn't finished. Please call me Xavier."

"Sure…Xavier."

"Don't you have another roommate?"

"Oh, she's out on a date, too. Just me by my lone-some. Me and my books," she said with a disappointed sigh. She extended her piece of pizza. The tip had been bitten off.

"Oh, no thanks. I'm about to eat dinner."

Then she realized she offered me a "used" piece. "I'm so sorry. Why don't you have a seat?"

"I'll go wait for Sophie in her room, if you don't

mind." The box in my coat pocket seemed heavier, but I managed to ignore it.

"Oh, sure."

On the way to Sophie's room, I noticed the bathroom door was open so I headed to her bedroom. I knocked and softly called her name.

The look on her face made me suck in my breath. She stood on the other side of the room in a silky, rose-colored robe that went to her mid-thighs. Her black hair was pinned up, but tendrils fell down her back, the tips of them wet from her shower.

"You're here early," was all she said.

"You're running behind," was my reply.

I approached her, my gaze hungry to see what lay underneath that robe. The opening to her robe parted, revealing the perfect curve to one breast. A jolt kicked my stomach as I watched water fall from her hair down between her breasts.

"I dress fast." She turned away from me, effectively blocking my view. Like she promised, she grabbed some clothes from her closet and put on a dress. Panties came next.

While she dressed, I took in her room. The space was small compared to the studio apartment bedroom, but everything had its place, from her tidied desk to all her cosmetics arranged by size on her vanity. A vase full of white flowers I didn't recognize sat next to what had to be her perfume. The scent from the perfume filled my nostrils and made my body ache.

Sophie briefly sat on her bed to open the bedside drawer. Her back was so elegant as she bent over to withdraw her leather cuffs. I sat beside her, but continued to face away from me. Did I upset her yesterday?

Quickly, she put on her cuffs, closed the drawer and used a key on her keyring to lock it.

So she had secrets…

I ran my fingers along the soft white petals to the green vines. The plant reminded me of the Morning Glory flowers my mother liked. "What is this?"

She glanced over her shoulder. "Moon flowers. They're my favorites. I managed to kidnap them back from Penny's room. That little thief waits for me to leave during the day."

Moon flowers.

"They're beautiful," I said.

"Definitely. Their true beauty is revealed a night."

Just like my Sophie. My thoughts flashed to the garden of night flowers and the way Sophie came undone as I touched her. I wanted to touch her like that again and hear soft moans, but this wasn't the time.

I shoved my hands into my pockets and pushed those thoughts elsewhere.

I circled her room again, this time stopping when I saw the marks on her white, metal bedpost. There were places on the outer bars where the paint had been scraped off to reveal the gray metal underneath.

I ran my fingers along the bedpost. "This is unusual."

She put on her shoes, not even giving me a side-glance. "It's an old bed."

Soon enough she grabbed her purse to leave. I grabbed her forearm.

"Is something wrong?" she asked.

"There's something I need to say before we go."

She paused and I gathered to strength to do something I hadn't done in a long time.

"We've only known each other for a short period of

time, but I feel like…" I tried to find the right words. "I feel like I've known you for a lot longer."

"Me, too."

"You're making it harder for me to want to finish this deal…"

Her eyes blinked in confusion. "What are you saying?"

"I like you, Sophie. I like you a lot." I placed my hand in my pocket and pulled out the box.

"What's that?" Her eyes grew wide.

Chapter Nineteen

Sophie

The dark red box was bigger than a ring box, that was for sure. Did I really want to open it though after all the things he said to me?

Intensity filled every feature of his face. His expression was similar to one he had at the bar, but this time the sharp edges along his strong chin were softer.

"Open it," he said.

I looked up at him again. He didn't blink once.

I pulled the top off the box to reveal two brand new leather cuffs. I couldn't resist touching them. Virgin light brown leather, soft as unmarred skin, with buckles and O rings made from 14K gold. I'd never felt anything smoother than the fleece lining on the inside.

"What's this?" I whispered.

Then I saw it. On the outside of each cuff were two initials, printed so tiny I had to squint: *X.Q.*

His mark.

I bit my lower lip, unsure of what to say.

I finally asked, "They're beautiful, but why did you do this?"

"It's a gift."

For a man who always said what he meant, this vague explanation grated my nerves. "Why did you…" I reached for the words, "Why are your initials on these?"

"Because I want you to be mine." His eyebrows lowered. *"I don't share."*

Hearing those words felt wonderful, but he shouldn't have done this. When Sato had given me my current pair of leather cuffs, there had been no pomp or circumstance. No formal collaring ceremony to tie me to him as his submissive. I was just a girl who got a pair of cuffs. Now, here I was standing in front of Xavier Quinn getting the same treatment.

This man would be here today, and most likely gone in the next. I had no reason to accept this.

Finding the right words made my throat dry. "We're not a couple. Why brand me as yours if you don't want a relationship?"

"It's just a gift."

No man puts his initials on a *gift.*

I put the cover over the box, effectively ending the subject. "Then thank you." I glanced at my watch.

"You don't like them?" He sounded surprised.

"They're beautiful, but I can't wear these right now."

He stiffened and a stone wall fell between us. I almost caught his look of hurt.

"Well, if we want to get there on time, we should leave now," he said a bit stiffly.

I nodded, unable to keep the harsh feeling from my stomach that no matter how much I didn't want to accept his gift, I'd done some very wrong. As we left my apartment, I suspected I'd never want anything from him again.

GUILT CONTINUED to weigh down my stomach as we entered a restaurant off of the bay. Was he still hurt?

During the whole trip, he walked beside me, but a barrier had fallen. Where before he'd place his hand on the middle of my back, he didn't do that anymore. When we reached the table, with a place setting for four, he did pull out my chair for me, but he didn't lean close to me.

So he was disappointed that I wouldn't wear them. *Tough.* Our arrangement worked if two people agreed to maintain our boundaries. He'd crossed that boundary the moment he gave me that cuff.

But, it is pretty, I admitted it to myself. *Would they be comfortable?*

I pushed those thoughts aside as Xavier took a seat beside me and didn't speak.

The waiter arrived and Xavier ordered a bottle of wine for us. Silence weighed heavy, even with all the diners around us having lively conversations. He was close enough to touch me if he only moved his right hand a few inches.

Just a few inches separated us, but it seemed like so much more.

I laughed a bit at the irony.

"What's so funny?" he finally asked me.

"This was all supposed to be easy, or maybe I thought it would be. We'd satisfy each other's needs during your time here." I shrugged. Things had become complicated. "And once you secured the contract you and I would move on. You to Arizona and me to London."

There, I said it. London seemed like the right decision at this point. What would keep me here in Boston other than my friends?

"Why London?" he placed his hand on his knee. If that hand was on my knee, he would be rubbing my flesh with the promise he'd go upward if I parted my thighs.

"My best friend, you remember me mentioning Carlie, right?"

He nodded.

"She's so strong. One of the strongest people that I know, but she has a weakness that makes me want to protect her." Just thinking about that tiny studio apartment I had with Carlie brought back feelings I liked to push aside. "Things have happened between us when we both were weak and she had to be the strong one. Now things have reversed. We've been friends for a long time and we take care of one another."

"Sounds like you two have quite a history."

"On my dark days, I feel like I'm wearing a mask. That I'm showing everyone the Sophie I want them to see. The strong person who is crumbling on the inside. Carlie is rarely that way. I'd do anything to protect her."

He nodded and reached out to touch my hand, only to pull away when two people approached us. I wiped away the tear that threatened to slip down my cheek.

The resemblance between the man and Xavier was apparent in their strong nose and chin. Compared to Xavier's assured walk, this man's approach was far more reserved. He had a slightly receding hairline and his eyebrows were a bit bushier. The woman beside him was refined typical of the wives married to affluent men: the salon styled hair, the virgin hands with manicured nails, the clothes that were conservative, yet expensive to show wealth and status.

She took one look at me and a slight grin tilted her lips.

Xavier stood and shook his brother's hand. No hug between them. Maybe they'd recently seen each other.

"You look good," the man said.

Xavier turned to me and introduced me to Marcus and his wife Becca.

I stood, prepared to take Becca's hand, but she scooted out her chair and took a seat eluding that formality. Well, that spoke volumes about what I should expect. I'd handled people like her before so I took my seat and added a smile to my face.

"The flight was delayed and we were stuck on the plane for two hours." Marcus groaned as they both shared a laugh.

"You always hated being late," Xavier said.

"No, Dad always hated when we were late," Marcus replied.

While they spoke, Marcus's wife beckoned the waiter over and ordered a bottle of wine for them. She said, and I quote, "I'd like something much *better* than what we have here."

Not one to be intimidated I spoke to her. "They look so alike. Do all his siblings look so similar?"

"I doubt it. Their sister is a girl." She tilted her head as if I was child misunderstanding the world.

How cute.

"I'm sure they're all attractive is what I meant. Have you been to Boston before?" I'd kill her with kindness. She'd suffer a coronary from it.

"Countless times. I hate Boston in the springtime. Any time of the year actually."

Marcus exchanged a glance with Xavier. One of exasperation. "I thought you like it here. You always begged me to bring you here for the marathon back when you ran."

"Well, I can't run anymore so what does it matter?"

Marcus held in an obvious sigh.

"You wanted to come to Boston, so I came with you. What more do you want?"

The tension between these two was about as thick as Xavier and myself. Although I'd admit at least I wouldn't pull this kind of mess in front of people who didn't know who I was.

"I want us to get along. The kids don't need to see us like this."

Xavier quickly interjected. "So how are my nieces and nephews?"

"They're driving my wife crazy. They all have a camp of some kind. Hayley has ballet camp. Heather has camp for orchestra and Mom is spoiling Regan and convinced us to let him go to Hawaii for a camp for marine wildlife studies."

Xavier chucked, although it sounded reserved. "That sounds like Mom. Always doing what she wants."

"Has she contacted you about her birthday party?" Becca asked, her fingers playing with the flute of her red wine glass.

Xavier rubbed his chin with his left hand. I saw him clench his right.

"I've always had other engagements. Why invite the family pariah when I have other things to do?"

"It doesn't have to be that way," Becca said, her tone turning harsh. "I've been a part of this family since you left college. You're about as stubborn as your mother."

Xavier's jaw twitched. His hand gripped his thigh hard enough for this knuckles to go white. I reached out with my left and touched his until he eased up.

"Seems like his stubborn streak has done him well. From what I hear, Xavier is about to secure the biggest deal of his career."

Becca's gaze focused on me.

"You're his new assistant, right?" So she was switching gears now. Poking at me for another vulnerable point. "The new Ian. Every assistant he has had before always was a man. He never wanted a woman so close. I guess this time he needed help in the office and in the bedroom."

"I think it's time for us to leave." Xavier prepared to stand, but I clenched his thigh this time. *Not so fast buddy.* I'd tangled with far crueler prey.

"I'm good at what I do, Mrs. Quinn. But what I excel at is handling people. I don't need to fling mud at others to compensate for my own insecurities or my own problems. I keep them at home."

Becca's grip on her drink tightened.

"I just wanted a few nights to forget," Marcus said to his wife. "Why are you stepping on my efforts?"

Marcus looked to us with an apologetic gaze. "I'm sorry about this. We should've eaten dinner alone."

"No need to apologize." Xavier looked to me and I took his cue that he was leaving even if he had to drag me out with him.

"It was a pleasure meeting you both." By the time we reached Atlantic Ave, I expected us to get into the car, but Xavier took my hand and we continued down the street heading north past the concrete storefronts. At this time of the evening, the city was still alive. Trollies passed us with wide-eyed tourists. People weaved around us to destinations unknown. It was just me and him, walking hand in hand.

We approached the aquarium.

"Have you ever been there before?" I asked him.

"Never had the chance."

"That's one of the first places I went when I first got here. Couldn't afford much else, but I could afford seeing the aquarium."

He smiled at me and I melted a bit.

We passed Tia's a long-standing tradition many clients asked me to visit during their stay. From there we reached Chris Columbus Park. He directed us toward the Harborwalk. I hadn't been here in a few months. I rarely came at night.

"This is nice," he remarked as we passed a man playing his guitar. Guess he was ready to talk now.

"Much nicer than the restaurant."

"I'm sorry about that."

I shrugged, ignoring the fact we were somehow holding hands, but maybe my touch was reassuring and comforting for him. "There's something going on between them. I understand and I've seen it before. When you're hurt you take things out on other people."

"Yeah, but that's not an excuse for her to mistreat you."

I shrugged again. "Be that as it may, I know what it's like to be sitting in her seat. When the world weighs down on you with your problems and you have no outlet, everyone gets to be as *happy* as you are." I did a single hand air quote for the word happy.

His hand tightened on mine. "You're not that way though."

"You've seen nice Sophie. Bitch Sophie will pull a knife on you and cut your ass."

He laughed this time.

Under normal circumstances, I'd never say such things in front of a client, but I'd exposed myself to Xavier in more ways than one. Why not show him down-to-earth Sophie?

"You got a knife on you now?"

I spotted a food truck selling tacos. "No, but I'm about to be armed and dangerous when it comes to fish tacos."

"That sounds good right about now."

We did miss out on dinner. "I don't know what kind of employer you are, letting your employees think they're going to get dinner and then you snatch the food away."

We got in line. "That was my plan the whole time." My stomach fluttered every time he looked at me like that. Like he enjoyed my company. Right now, with his hand in mine and mine in his, it was natural, like we did this every time we went out in public.

"I need to keep you working hard," he added.

"Is that right?" We reached the end of the line and ordered our tacos. I offered to pay, but he declined and took care of our meals.

We found a bench nearby and dug into our food. Even though we ate in silence, I couldn't stop smiling.

"What is it?" he asked, his mouth full of food.

"It's weird to be honest."

"Why?" he took a sip of his drink.

"I'm sitting next to the owner of Silver Sparrow Systems eating ten dollar tacos."

"And?"

"You can be intimidating without trying hard."

He offered me a grin beautiful enough to make me want to kiss him. Oh, how I wanted kiss him.

I took my napkin and wiped off his mouth instead. He reached up and took my hand. Our gazes locked and my heart sputtered from the heat of his gaze. All I'd wanted was one touch.

I tried to pull away, but he took the napkin from me and placed my hand on his cheek. Damn him and the perfect stubble on his cheeks. Using his other free hand he grasped my other one and placed it on this other cheek. His lips parted and my imagination ran wild. Heat filled my core when he took my right hand and ran my fingertips along his lower lip. Then he kissed my fingertips.

This was dangerous, but damn it was what I needed. I wanted more than one touch. I wanted to be in his bed tonight. No matter how much regrets went through my head about his leaving, me leaving, or his gift to replace my cuffs.

What I had left after I cast those doubts aside was this glorious feeling. Something I'd missed for so long. Lust didn't make lean forward to brush my lips against his. Longing didn't make me grab the lapel of his shirt to keep him close. It had to be love.

He tasted like the sauce from the tacos. Quite tasty.

"You taste good," I murmured against his mouth.

"Still hungry?" he asked.

"Not for food."

I sucked in a breath, the one he exhaled. "You too?"

He pulled out his phone and made a call. "Chris, Miss Ashton and I are ready to go home now."

Chapter Twenty

Xavier

As much as I thought I'd be prepared for a call from Nakamura's assistant, I wasn't ready. Even more so eager he'd arranged for us to meet at Nakamura's suite at the Ritz Carlton.

It was time for me to have my moment and all my confidence was threatening to leave me.

If anyone would've asked me any aspect of my plan, I would have confidently given them enough detail to put their ass to sleep. But this time nervousness made my palms sweaty and my stomach jumpy.

Chris dropped me off at the hotel early so I could be there on time. I'd checked in with my team at Silver Sparrow and everything was a go. If he agreed to work with my people, we'd be ready. Was I hyping up everything for nothing?

Last night with Sophie had been good for me. After exposing my heart to her and then having Becca attempt to ridicule me, having a night with Sophie all to myself had been great.

Our bodies had intertwined last night in more positions than pretzel formations. My body hummed in remembrance from her mouth on me. The way she licked me from my earlobe down to my cock. I got her back though. I had her screaming out my name until the neighbors probably knew who I was.

The elevator chimed that I'd reached my floor.

This was it.

I knocked on the door and his assistant answered. As Sophie instructed I checked to see if shoes had been left near the door. None were there so I kept my shoes on and followed Nakamura's assistant Ichiro. The suite was well-decorated with fresh flowers and dark mahogany decor. I was led into the main great room where Nakamura was reading a newspaper on the wide balcony.

Instead of taking in the amazing view, I extended my right hand, grasping my wrist with my left. Nakamura gave me a firm handshake as I bowed.

"I'm glad you came," he said.

"I'm pleased you took the time from your busy schedule to see me."

We sat down at the balcony table and his assistant poured me tea.

"You're quite persistent, Mr. Quinn," Nakamura remarked.

"In this business you have to be, but there are times when persistence can get a man into trouble."

"Truly."

He was silent for a moment and I wondered what I should say. Most certainly pitching the proposal my lawyers had sent him so long ago seemed too bold.

"I've read your proposal and you have intriguing

ideas," Nakamura said.

Now that almost knocked me off my feet. "Thank you."

"But I don't know if you're the man to do them. You seem to be on a train without brakes. A boat sailing off into the unknown."

I'd been told this before. "Mr. Nakamura, you have the resources and experience I need. I'm willing to learn and I'm willing to do whatever is necessary to show you I'm the best."

Nakamura nodded for me to continue. I had my shot now. It was up to me to cross the finish line.

~

A FEW DAYS PASSED.

I was at the gym working out when a phone call came in from Ian in Phoenix. "We've received news with an offer to sit down and begin the negotiation process for a contract."

I grinned from ear to ear. "Good to hear you sounding better."

"I thought I was going to have to send out a search party for my lung, Mr. Quinn." Ian had sounded like a hung-over smoker who'd been dragged through a metal grate.

Ian fed me what little details existed: I was needed back in Arizona to begin the process and everything would be waiting for me when I got there.

The contract could wait though. I planned to get out of these sweaty clothes so I could go see Sophie and cele-brate. She'd be overjoyed to hear about our victory. I shrugged off my sweats when my phone rang again. Prob-ably Ian to nag me to hurry up.

But when I picked up the phone, I was surprised to see Marcus' number.

"You still having fun in Boston?" I asked.

"I'm not in Boston anymore." The withdrawn sound of my brother's voice made me pause.

"What's going on, Marcus? Is everything all right with Mom and Dad?"

He sighed. "It's not them. It's Becca. She has cancer."

The weight of his words forced me back to my bed. I sat down with a heavy heart. "Marcus…"

"We've been hiding this from everyone. Maybe we hoped we could hide her treatment from the kids. From everybody for as long as possible, but she's gotten sicker and now she needs me to be there for her."

"I'm so sorry." Marcus had bared the burdens of our family for so long. The vacation resort business, the expectations of my parents. "I hate saying this, but I need you back home. I have people I trust, but I don't trust them like I trust you."

I ran my hands through my hair, unable to imagine the shit my brother was going through. Why hadn't I been nicer to Becca? "You can count on me."

"Yeah?"

"I'd planned to return to the west coast anyway."

"What about the girl I saw you with? Your assistant, or should I say girlfriend?"

Now that was another matter I'd have to settle. "I don't know if she wants to take what we have to the next level or not, but I'd like to see where things go." Something swelled inside my chest. A good feeling I hadn't felt since I'd last been with Sophie.

Maybe this was the sign I'd been waiting for to do what was right.

Chapter Twenty-One

Sophie

I heard from Komiko sooner than I'd expected. I would be seeing Sato again. A few days wasn't enough time for the news to sink in though.

Staring at the text message didn't help:

Sato is waiting for you at the Moko's Sushi Bar.

The message was simple, yet my heart dropped every time I glanced at my phone. Knowing he was in town was hard enough, but knowing he waiting to see me made a familiar ache in my chest return.

If I was still hurting, why was I on my way to Southie? Instead of taking a cab, I took the train to South Boston instead. I needed time—a lot of it—to prepare for what was about to happen.

This trip was a familiar one. The blue line to the orange one. From there it was a bus ride toward City Point. Every minute was a journey to a place from a different time. A happier time. Two years ago, before he'd left, we'd held hands going down E Broadway, past the Medal of

Honor Park, on the way to Moko's. In the wintertime, snowdrifts gathered along the roads, but that didn't stop us from trudging there.

I sighed. Now that I stood in front of Moko's, I was happier, but in a different way. I was ready to see Sato, even though my body churned in agony—almost as if my spine remembered the pain of crying for days.

I straightened my back and opened the door. Moko's hadn't changed much since my last visit. The décor still welcomed anyone with its rustic, down home feel. None of the chairs or tables was made of plastic. All the chairs were lived-in and there were tears in the fabric on the seats, but, based on experience I knew I'd feel at home. Hiruto, the owner's son, was still working behind the counter cooking food, while his wife Carmine was taking orders at the register. In a way, Komiko had chosen a spot where I'd been confident and carefree.

The last time I'd walked into this place I'd been happy. I could still be that Sophie.

He was in our spot. The corner booth nearest to the door.

Sato didn't turn to look at me. Even when I slipped into the seat and placed my tote bag on the floor. A meal was waiting for me though. A California sushi roll wrapped with extra seaweed. So he remembered.

"How are you?" he began. That simple statement from him held so many meanings.

He was still as beautiful as I remembered, but his face was a bit thinner. The power in his dark gaze remained. Somehow just sitting in front of him, I felt smaller.

He glanced at my wrists. I wasn't wearing his leather cuffs. Nor did I have plans to do that anymore.

"Much better after you left. I'm well." I placed the napkin in my lap. Then using the chopsticks, I placed the first piece in my mouth. So many wonderful tastes crossed my tongue.

"You look well." He paused, watching me eat. "Thank you for meeting me."

I shrugged. "Even after what you did to me, I know how to be civil."

"I appreciate that." Another long pause. "For the longest of time, I've tried to think of what to say to you if I ever had an opportunity like this."

Had an opportunity? My bite came down hard. A real man would have come to my face and admitted what he'd done.

Sato continued. "But there's nothing I can say to make amends, other than see you today." Sincerity filled his features. Two years ago, I would've tossed my water into his face, but today I just nodded so I could say what I should have said so long ago.

"Leaving me behind was so…fucked up…and you know I rarely say that word out loud…that I've done things I never would've done before. I've closed myself off from people. People who would've loved me and accepted me for who I was." I kept talking, even though my throat had gone dry and my fists clenched so tightly they hurt. But I didn't cry—I was past crying and there was nothing left. "You took something so *beautiful* between us and you were too much of a *fucking* coward to let me go."

He accepted my venom, not saying a word the whole time. This was the Sato I remembered. Stone. Unmoving. Once I was done speaking, he finally spoke. "Shame followed me home to Hiroshima and continues to follow me, Sophie. I'm trying to make amends."

"With your little gifts?" I took the tote bag and placed it at his feet under the table. "You can have them back. Stop sending them to me."

"I will do that if it's what you want," he said.

"Does your fiancée know about your shame? Your gifts?" I asked him.

"No, she doesn't. It's for the best."

I snorted. Shouldn't be surprised. "You better do well by her."

He nodded, his hands still in his lap. Sato had always been bold, commanding. Every move he made was certain, seemingly calculated. Now that I had scolded him, he was silent.

A question circled my tongue and I wanted to hold it back, but I couldn't. "Did you ever love me?"

He took a deep breath. "What I can say is I loved the moments we shared." He paused as if pensive. "I've never met a woman like you before. You're responsive. Sensual. Everything I could've wanted in a partner, but as hard as we tried, my parents would have never accepted an American. A life beyond what we had was impossible."

Impossible? Just impossible for him.

At that moment, I should've got up and left, but damn it I came here to eat Moko's food. I wouldn't *let* him force me to leave. So I picked up my chopsticks again. Might as well get a free meal of out of this. I'd learned all I needed to know.

When I finished eating, I even put my hand up for the waitress so I could make another order. "I'd like two more California roll meals to go. Put them on *his* bill, please."

When the sack arrived with the meals, I got and left. I didn't say a damn word. Why bother with saying goodbye? Sato didn't believe in them.

∾

Xavier

Endless calls kept me from seeing Sophie all day. Never would I have imagined that I'd be overseeing the company that I'd run away from most of my adult life.

Instead of feeling jubilant as I walked up the stairs to Sophie's apartment, I was apprehensive.

I'd called Sophie's cell a few times over an hour ago, but she hadn't answered, so I called her apartment. One of her roommates, the one named Penny, picked up the phone.

"So you're looking for Sophie?" A slight pause. "Yeah, Ashley's here. She came home a few hours ago and then went straight to bed. It's really weird."

"Who's *Ashley*?"

Penny laughed, her voice melodious and smooth. "She never told you she changed her name, huh? I've always known her as Ashley." Her voice dropped as if she wanted to share more secrets. "I'll let you ask her about it after she wakes up and calls you back."

"Is she all right?" I asked.

"I don't know. She hardly *ever* sleeps. She sleeps like three to four hours a night like clockwork."

Sophie couldn't be mad at me, we'd parted on good terms the last time we'd seen each other. "Can you let me in if I come by to see her?"

"If you knock, I'll answer."

So here I was. It was almost ten o'clock, but I didn't care.

In the darkness of her bedroom, I couldn't make out much, just her silent form on the bed. She seemed so vulnerable while she was curled up on her side. Her breaths were even—she was sleeping peacefully.

I dueled with the idea of leaving, but I missed her so I

took off my shoes and joined her in the bed. The mattress groaned a bit, but she didn't stir. I settled behind her and wrapped my left arm around her waist. She was wonderfully warm, smelling of her fruity shampoo. I ran my nose along the crown of her head. *Heaven.* My groin tightened just thinking about what she might not be wearing. The longer I lay next to her, the more peace settled in my bones.

Then Sophie spoke. "When did you get here?"

So she was awake.

"Not too long ago." I kissed the back of her head. We fit so perfectly together.

"Did you get the contract?" she asked, her voice still a bit sleepy.

I ran my hands down her extended arms to her hands —then I noticed she wore her leather cuffs. A chain linked them to the bed.

Now this was unexpected.

"What's this?" I asked softly. She was all alone. Why was she wearing these?

She paused as if she considered what she was about to say. "I needed them tonight. For the *last* time." She shifted and I caught the sounds of her removing the cuffs.

A weight lifted from my chest. Did that mean she was getting rid of them? "Why do you wear them by yourself?"

I'd yet to meet any sub who did self-bondage.

Placing them on the nightstand, she turned around to face me. Her lips brushed against mine. "Sometimes I wear them for comfort. I guess you could say they're like an anchor. A reminder of the pleasure I experienced during a scene."

"Scenes with Sato? Do you *reminisce* being with him?" I didn't want her thinking about him anymore.

"I have new memories now. With you." She shivered so

I rubbed her arms. "You're quite good at helping me create great ones."

Satisfied with her response, I stroked her back and we fell into a comfortable silence.

Before I drifted off to sleep, she ended the silence with her original question. "Did you get the contract?"

"Not exactly, but the first step in the negotiation process has begun. Our lawyers will be meeting at the end of this week…Ashley."

She snorted.

"So when did you plan to tell me you're Ashley Ashton?" I asked.

"How about never? I've nuked every document with that name, but Carlie and Penny won't let my birth name die a good death."

I relaxed again and looked forward to every opportunity I'd get to tease her. The name was sexy as hell. I could get used to lying next to her in bed like this. Tension filled my limbs and my hunger for her was peaking again. "I never imagined I'd reach this point. From the beginning, I thought I'd have to beg on my knees and fling every achievement I had at him. In the end, all it took was one conversation. A confession and an admission."

Her head tilted. "An admission?"

"I admitted my imperfections and I confessed you're the reason I made it this far. I was supposed to show up here with flowers, but Ian is running a bit late."

She laughed a bit. "So Ian's well again? I guess he can make your flight arrangements."

"I'd like it if my flight back home included *two* people instead of one."

Her head turned sharply toward me. "What are you saying?"

"Come to Arizona with me. My brother's wife Becca is ill and Marcus needs my help with the family's company."

A wave of emotions crossed her face in the darkness. Uncertainty. Sadness at hearing about Becca. With little light all I could see was the rapid blink of her eyes and her parted mouth.

"You don't have to decide right now," I said to reassure her. "Just come for the weekend and see if you want to stay with me."

For a while, she didn't say anything. Doubts circled my mind, too. Memories of Rosalie was strongest back there and as much as I wanted Sophie with me, the idea of bringing a woman to the home I was supposed to make with Rosalie fed those doubts. I needed a new start as badly as Sophie did.

"Just a weekend," she finally said. "Nothing more?"

I slowly nodded. One weekend for us both. "You've given me everything I could ever need in Boston. I should return the favor." Unable to resist, I cupped her breast through the thin material.

"What are you doing?"

"Just getting comfortable..." My cock was aching at this point. "I'm thinking I should supervise your packing in the morning to make sure you don't back out. I'd like to leave tomorrow morning if possible."

She was so soft, so sweet. She moaned as my hand ran down her belly to seek out the warmth between her thighs.

"From now on I'll be the one who comforts you," I whispered. I pulled up her arms upward, stretching them until her back arched. Every night she'd been with me, she'd slept well. By the time I was done with her tonight, she'll sleep in long enough for us to miss any morning flight.

Chapter Twenty-Two

Sophie

Not sure how this happened, but instead of flying east to London, I was flying west to Arizona. Just for the weekend anyway.

I was flying all alone, too. To my surprise Xavier had to fly out earlier today to handle business at Silver Sparrow Systems. I smiled at the thought of his face when he told me he was going home to work on negotiations with Naka-mura. *He'd done it.* And I'd been there with him through it all.

So what now, though? As I got off the jet at the Phoenix Sky Harbor International Airport into the dry, Arizona heat, I asked myself that question. Back when I was with Sato, I had dreams of stepping off the plane in Japan. I remembered the growing excitement in my belly and all the hopes and dreams I had of meeting his family. For the first time I would be dropkicked into a place where I hadn't prepared for a visit beforehand.

Case in point, I was barely prepared for anything today

and it was my job to be prepared. Not that I hadn't done a little bit of research. *Don't get me wrong.* I was good at what I did for a reason, but this time things were different. I was the visiting girlfriend this time and not the client.

Xavier was about to have a great deal on his plate with over fifteen resorts from Arizona to southern California. In addition to handling duties at Silver Sparrow Systems, he'd be overseeing a company with hundreds of employees and whatever issues Marcus left him to deal with.

Outside of the jet, a black Bentley waited for me and I smiled to see Chris behind the wheel.

"Welcome to Phoenix, Miss Ashton," Chris said with a smile.

"Thanks! Good to see you. Are we going to his place?"

"No, we won't be going to Mr. Quinn's home in the city until after dinner. I was told to take you to the Quinn family compound in Mayer."

I got into the backseat, again thrown off and unsure what was about to happen. Not once did he tell me about meeting the rest of his family.

This is a good sign, Sophie, I told myself. *He's serious us about us.*

Meeting Sato's family had been hard, but I'd survived the affairs with a smile.

The drive was wonderful though. I'd never been to Arizona before, much less the southwest. I'd been to southern California countless times for business, but the landscape here was breathtaking. Outside of the airport we drove northward along the Black Canyon Freeway, past the suburbs and skyscrapers toward the countryside. Endless earth tones dotted the landscape and I fell into the view. I couldn't wait to see the sunsets and sunrises out here.

Finally, we reached our final destination. When Chris had said 'family compound' he wasn't kidding. After one hour of driving, we'd reached a long driveway that led to a gated fence with a security guard. The guard let us through, and soon enough, we approached a vast two-level mansion with beautiful windows and grey stonework along the front. The cobblestone driveway even had a double fountain.

"You can tell how rich your customers are by the number of fountains they have in front of their house. It shows how much water they can afford to waste on a daily basis," Carlie used to say.

We were in the desert and they had two of them. I stifled a giggle.

"Everything fine, Miss Ashton?" Chris asked as he pulled to a stop.

"Oh, everything's good. Just taking it all in."

He nodded with a small smile. He was probably used to seeing this house and every other place Xavier had been before.

Just another day with the filthy rich.

An older man, who looked to be nor more than fifty with blondish-white hair, opened the door for me. Soon enough I was out of the dry heat and into the massive foyer, which technically still could be considered outside.

The foyer had another fountain.

"I'm Yates," the man who led me said. "Miss Ashton, it's a pleasure to have you here. The Quinn family always meets at five for dinner. I asked the kitchen to prepare some tea and refreshments."

"Thank you for the warm welcome." There was no one was around to welcome me though. I did hear sounds of laughter and others' voices. I pushed the thought away and followed Yates.

I was led through the house, going down countless hallways until we reached a suite the size of my apartment. This place was amazing.

"Please rest here for the afternoon before dinner. I hope your accommodations are acceptable?" Yates asked.

Were there people who said they weren't?

"Of course, this is lovely."

"If there is anything you need please use the phone and hit the star button to reach the staff."

It was like this place was a hotel.

"Do you have any questions?" he asked before he left.

"Actually I do if you don't mind?"

He nodded, probably not expecting me to have any.

I was on a different battleground now, but one thing I learned from my industry was that the staff lived on the frontlines and if I wanted to things to start off right, I needed to be prepared. Xavier threw me off my game when he didn't tell me about dinner with the Quinns. "Does Xavier's mother like gifts?"

Yates's eyebrow rose. "Mrs. Quinn likes gifts, but she can be particular in what she likes."

Not too much information. He was loyal and that was good. Time to dig deeper.

"Someone as nice as Mrs. Quinn probably donates gifts like paintings, hand-written items to the hospitals." I took in the room while I spoke. It was good to keep things casual.

"Mrs. Quinn has always been a fervent supporter of the local animal shelters. She loves to donate stuffed animals to shelters and flowers to the sick at the local hospital."

So he narrowed it down for me. Very nice.

I turned toward him. "She sounds like a gem. Thanks for your help."

His smile widened. My first potential ally. "Where would you like your tea and sandwiches?" On the balcony or the sitting area?"

~

MY NEW ALLY DIDN'T PREPARE ME for what was to come at dinnertime. Xavier had yet to arrive and I was on my own.

I got a text message as I followed a maid down the stairs to the dining room: *almost there. can't wait to see you.*

My heart fluttered a bit. We'd only been apart less than a day, yet I couldn't wait to be with him again. Was this what normal relationships felt like?

The noise level rose as I reached the dining room and then a hand closed over my wrist and gently pulled me around a corner.

"Hey," I called out, only to have my lips covered by Xavier's. His large hand caressed the back of my head and couldn't help but collapse against him.

"Mmmm," he said against my mouth. "You taste good."

I turned to see the maid I was following had disappeared.

"Aren't we expected for dinner?" I could still hear his family down the hall. They were quite loud.

He ran his hands down my back and kissed my neck. "They're not going anywhere until all the food is gone. My aunt's a really good cook."

"Oh, is she?"

Footsteps approached from around the corner. Xavier took my hand and quickly added space between us.

Marcus peeked his head around the corner. "There you are." He saw his brother and cocked a grin. "Don't keep Mom waiting. You two can do *that* later."

Heat filled my face.

Xavier groaned. "All I did was kiss her. You didn't miss anything."

He pulled me behind him, our hands still intertwined. As we entered the dining room, the confident Sophie slinked away under the curious gazes of over fifteen people in the huge dining room.

Quinn Compound, I reminded myself.

There were too many people to track so I pasted a smile on my face and tried to look friendly.

Put your hand up and wave, I reminded myself. Like a robot I put my hand in the air. When I noticed how slow I was going I went too fast.

Two women, who had to be his aunts, exchanged glances.

You know how to impress 'em like a pro, Sophie.

A bunch of kids ran to us and Xavier released my hand to pick up twin girls on each arm.

"Daddy said you were staying with us for a while since Mommy is sick," one said, her pigtails bouncing up and down.

"Yeah, I'm helping your daddy out." He adjusted them on each arm. "I don't know if Heather's getting heavier or is it Hayley?"

They giggled and I saw their mother behind Xavier.

My heart clenched to see Becca sitting at the table. Her hair was different from what I'd seen at the restaurant. And then it hit me: she'd been wearing a wig.

She glanced up at me and offered a smile. I smiled back.

"Who's this?" Hayley asked.

"This is Sophie," Xavier said.

"Your girlfriend?" Heather said with a grin.

He whispered with a devilish grin into their ears and they laughed.

"Hey," I said, "What secret are you three keeping?"

I didn't get a reply as more kids overwhelmed their

poor uncle. Seeing Xavier like this, with his nieces and nephews made my heart melt.

By the time everyone sat down, another thing was quite apparent. No one else had acknowledged me other than the kids, Becca, and Marcus. Although it was hard to see around the table though. At least twenty to thirty people found a place to sit. My spot was next to Xavier near the head of the table.

The family matriarch sat at the head. Xavier definitely took after her. They had the same beautiful blond hair and light blue eyes.

"How was your flight?" his mother asked him as the house staff placed a bowl of vegetable soup in front of everyone.

"Nothing special." Xavier even shrugged, but didn't look at her. Would all their conversations progress like this?

"Have you had a chance to meet with the executive team yet?" she asked. No hey, 'how are you doing'? Just straight to resort business.

"I've had a conference call with Steven, but I'm not too concerned," Xavier replied. "We need to use our resources. Steven would've been a great person to handle things."

Mrs. Quinn's severe bob gave her a sharp edge. "You know how we are. We don't let *anyone* outside of the family handle things."

"I know how you are, Mom," Xavier murmured after he took a bite of vegetables from his soup.

She glanced at him briefly, the critical look in her eyes dimming for a moment. "You could come here more often, you know."

"I see Marcus and his family pretty often."

Ouch. That hurt even me. If I had a mother, I'd do anything to spend quality time with her.

The tension rising at this end of the table didn't affect anyone else. They kept on eating and chatting. To settle things down, I spoke. "You have beautiful home, Mrs. Quinn."

"Thank you." She sipped her wine and then gave me a tight-lipped smile.

Keep smiling, Sophie. "I saw you have a Mansour in the great room. I love his work."

The Quinn matriarch put down her wine. "I think I need to make something clear, Miss?"

I opened my mouth to speak, but Xavier beat me.

"Mom—" Xavier began. "You promised me."

My smile wanted to die, but I kept on smiling, knowing a train wreck was about to happen. And all before I had a chance to offer her the gift I wanted to give her after prying the valuable information from Yates. Slowly, I slide the box into the pocket of my dress. *Not a good time for flattery, Ashton.*

"My son never brings his *women* here," she said crisply. "The last time he did a few years ago, he thought it was funny to bring one of his *playthings*."

Xavier's hand tightened around his napkin.

She continued and I had to bite my inner cheek to stay silent. I knew very well what she meant by playthings. His kinky playthings. "That's why I've been trying to find him a *nice* girl for once."

"I'm not in the mood for this," Marcus grumbled.

"As the leader of this family, I need to know where you stand," she said point blank.

Xavier turned to me, clearly annoyed. "You don't have to answer, Sophie. Matter of fact, we're leaving."

"No, it's fine." Then I said to Mrs. Quinn, "I'm many things, but I'm not a plaything." I took a moment to lick my dry lips. "I am open book. Ask anything you like. I was raised in the foster system after my mother abandoned me in a hospital in the Bronx. I lived on the streets after I was eighteen. Right now I'm an elite personal concierge in Boston and I'm more capable than most people you'd meet. Like you, Mrs. Quinn, I don't need someone—namely a man—to do what I want to do."

Not far from me, I caught Becca grinning from ear to ear.

Mrs. Quinn stared at me for a bit, perhaps considering my response. I'd told her the truth. If she couldn't accept that, it was her loss and not mine. Finally, when she picked up her soup to begin eating again, I let out a long sigh of relief.

Dinner after that was quiet and strained. One of Xavier's uncles tried to crack a few jokes, but they were met with a frost reception. It was as if Mrs. Quinn's mood bled to everyone else.

Except the kids, at least laughed and joked among themselves.

Dinner ended, but I didn't eat much of my enchiladas. They were quite good, but I could find my appetite.

As everyone began to leave the table to retire for the night, Becca approached me. "I'm sorry about the last time we met."

"I appreciate your apology." I grinned at her and the smile she returned was genuine.

"Feeling miserable is no excuse to take out my anger on another party." She looked at her husband. "I'm going through a tough time right now with Marcus and Mom isn't help things."

"Having a family is never easy. I wish I had relatives."

"Oh, I'm sorry. I hadn't meant to bring up family like that—"

I offered her a wide grin. "I have a new family now and

they're great." I smiled thinking of Griff, Carlie and Penny. Naturally, I wondered if we'd still keep in contact if I moved to London. I pushed those thoughts away. I was with Xavier right now and I should enjoy the moment.

Becca glanced at her mother-in-law. "I wanted to put her in her place for the last fifteen years. How did you manage to do it on the first night?"

I hadn't put her in her place by a *long* shot in my opinion. "You'd be surprised what you're capable of doing after you've been asked to serve the moon on a plate the size of a silver thimble."

We began to walk for a bit and she showed me around the family pictures. Marcus and his brother were adorable as little kids. I even found out Xavier liked to run around naked when he was a toddler. Hope filled my chest, leaving me smiling like a fool. All these pictures gave me something I wanted to hold onto dearly: maybe I'd have a family like this someday. Don't get me wrong, I did have Carlie, Penny, and Griff, but I didn't want to be single forever. Someday I wanted a kid or two. Maybe find a nice place to settle down near a beach. I've done so much travelling in my life and I couldn't keep this lifestyle forever.

I turned to see Mrs. Quinn standing on the other side of the room chatting with one of Xavier's aunts. The smile on her face faded and a cold visage marred her beautiful features. With that one look, the airy feeling in my heart was sucked away.

Welcome to Phoenix, Sophie.

Chapter Twenty-Three

Xavier

The trip into downtown Phoenix was a quiet, somber one. At this time of the night, the skyscrapers cast a glow on the evening sky. The beautiful sight outside was difficult to enjoy with the tension blanketing my body.

During the whole time, I faced the window, my body turned away from Sophie.

She probably wondered if she'd done something wrong. Maybe she assumed my mother was the cause—which wasn't too off base most of the time. Every now and then, Sophie furtively glanced in my direction, but most of the time, she took in the view outside the window. If I was polite I should've ask her what she thought of Phoenix. I should've welcomed her here.

Instead I kept bunching my fists and fought the need to wipe the sweat gathering on my palms. My stomach quivered. Thoughts circled my mind up to the point where Chris entered my building's private parking garage: *What the hell was I doing bringing another woman into the space I made for Rosalie?*

Rosalie's gone, I immediately reminded myself as we came to a stop.

But her absence didn't change what was about to happen.

Sophie got out of the car first, turning to me with a grin. "Is this whole building yours?"

"Yes."

"Looks nice."

"Thank you." I was up to two words now. I was making progress.

I led her from the parking garage to a private elevator. The gilded steel doors beckoned us, opening up based on the key card I had on me.

"This is amazing!" Her gaze swept over the expansive elevator cab with the stainless steel bars and clear glass on the floor.

"The clear glass is a dare," Rosalie had said when we rode in the elevator for the first time six years ago. *"When boundaries like this are removed, you're forced to face your mortality."*

On that particular day, as we rose to the second floor, she stopped the elevator. With a coy smile, Rosalie descended to her knees and opened my pants to free my cock. I took in her beautiful face as she pleasured me to completion.

Today, I didn't dare look down.

"What kind of floor is this?" Sophie gasped.

"Plexiglas."

She pressed herself against me and focused on my face, a giggle escaping her mouth. "Wow. How do you go up and down this thing without looking down?"

"Gotten used to it I guess."

Not every part of this building had Rosalie's personal

touch. The first five floors included office space for the smaller companies Silver Sparrow Systems has acquired over the years, as well as a boutique space on the ground floor. But coming back here stirred memories I'd pushed away for a long time.

We reached the penthouse, and once the doors opened, I led her inside.

Everything was as I'd left my home over a month ago. Not a single thing out of place in the open concept penthouse. But each spot held memories from the study to the kitchen. We ate breakfast and argued politics in the mornings next to the windows overlooking the mountains. Her favorite spot in the room was the alcove next to my book collection.

Once she was diagnosed with giant cell myocarditis, everything changed. She grew too tired to do anything. The couch where we used to sit side-by-side with our laptops became the place where she slept. The bed where we played out scene after scene became the place I held her, hoping her heart would continue to beat until a donor heart became available.

Countless specialists, the best that money could buy, kept warning me that due to her enlarged heart she could die at any moment, but when she suddenly passed away I wasn't ready.

I was one of the richest men in the world, yet I couldn't even save a woman who didn't love me as deeply as I loved her.

This home had too many painful memories, but taking Sophie to a hotel was out of the question and a man like me never backed down from a challenge. It was time for me to face this issue head on.

"Take a look around," I said to Sophie. "Make yourself at home."

Sophie

If Xavier's place in Back Bay had left me floored, this one left me breathless.

"This is so beautiful." My gaze swept over the grey-tiled walls to the burnt orange drapes along the tall, yet narrow windows. This wasn't a bachelor's home. This was a showcase in craftsmanship with exquisite detail. So many leatherbound books filled custom bookcases. And the artwork! When Xavier said he enjoyed Klimt, that had only been a hint as to his affinity for the arts. I spied four paintings in the living room alone. I couldn't identify them, but the quality boasted his wealth.

Instead of walking around, I reached out to touch the leather chairs. I'd never seen such a style before. A stripe of black leather ran from the top of the seat down the middle. Smooth grey cotton on the rest of the seat added a softness to the hard edge of the leather.

"Those were custom made in Switzerland," he said from behind me.

I snorted from his casual comment. "Custom furniture from Europe?" I guess did that all the time with my IKEA stuff.

The whole vibe seemed modern to me, yet sleek.

"How long did it take for you to decorate this place?" I asked.

"A year and a half."

"Where did you live before then?"

"For the longest of time I stayed in my first condo. Before I made it big with Silver Sparrow I lived in a two-bedroom condo near campus. With not the tidiest of neighbors I might add."

"The joys of college campus living." I weaved around his furniture, a glint of light catching my eye. "Now this is different." I picked up a heavy, yet gorgeous crown made out of metal. Intricate etchings swirled along the outside.

"Be careful." Xavier reached in to take it from me, but not before I caught the engraved text chiseled in small letters along the inside.

Every king deserves a crown. I bow before you. From Rosalie.

Now that was unusual. "I wasn't going to break it," I said softly.

His serious expression faded quickly.

"It's rather fragile."

A metal crown was fragile? That polished metal had to be titanium. Now this was new one. I opened my mouth to ask who Rosalie was, but he took my hand and led me into the kitchen.

A kitchen twice the size of my bedroom. We passed two stoves on the way to the stainless steel fridge.

"You hungry?" he asked.

"Not really. Like you said, your aunt is a really good cook." The zipper on my pants would cry out mercy if I ate anything else.

I watched with curiosity as he gathered together vanilla ice cream, whipped cream, sour cream, strawberries, and a small bottle of brandy.

"What are you making?" I asked.

"You'll see." He tapped the granite top counter. "Have a seat."

While he mixed together the ice cream, whipped cream, and sour cream, I checked my text messages, only to learn Jesse had a few issues for me to handle. Another day, another diva. By the time I glanced up, he had two glasses of sliced strawberries prepared. He poured the cream mixture on top of the strawberries. I couldn't wait to sample what he prepared for us.

Instead of handing me a glass though, he took a spoon from a drawer, and scooped out a portion. The slight curve to the side of his mouth spoke volumes of his naughty intentions.

"I can't have my own?" I asked. My phone buzzed with a message, but I ignored it.

"No strawberries Romanov for you yet." He edged in between my legs, his left hand traveling up my thigh, while his right hand brought the serving toward my mouth. I opened wide—only to have him smear the cream along my jaw.

"Hey—" I swallowed my protest when his mouth sucked away the food, leaving sparks along the sensitive skin on my neck. Over and over he teased me with a taste, only to leave a bit of cream here and there. By the fifth time, I managed to steal a bite.

He stole a kiss instead.

That single long kiss wasn't heated or frenzied like in past. It was slow and measured. His lips gliding over mine. Our kiss grew heated and I couldn't help but drown in the sensations I experienced: the sweetness of the strawberries Romanov I sampled, the saltiness of his skin on my tongue, and tingles along my spine. His free hand holding the crown of my head to hold me in place while he swallowed my soul whole.

I liked this relaxed Xavier Quinn.

He ran his hand down my leg. I quivered from his touch. "I want you to stay with me," he whispered.

I flinched. Stopping myself wasn't possible.

"Just hear me out, Sophie. I'll setup your business on the west coast. You'll have your own office space, everything." He kissed my shoulder and my skin sang from the attention.

How I wanted to give into the fantasy. My own corner office. A staff to help me manage unruly clients. But reality hovered and pecked at me. What about my friends in Boston? All my business connections wouldn't be as valuable. Distance was a factor when dealing with people who liked seeing your face.

I'd be starting from scratch.

You'd be starting from scratch if you moved to London, I reminded myself.

A cold chill coursed down my back. The very idea of having nothing scared the hell out of me.

If I went to London, I'd have Carlie and all her clients, but I wouldn't have him anymore.

His words pierced me, but I forced them to flow through me. I had to. This weekend wasn't a promise but a chance for me to think things through.

"I need time," I finally said.

He nodded and fed me another bite. I wouldn't be deterred though, no matter how much my heart wanted me to stay. Loving him was far too easy of a thing to do.

When he reached back to get another scoop, I snatched the spoon from his hand. "My turn."

But he wasn't going down with a fight. We laughed, giggled, and snorted, our arms flying madly about to control the spoon. He tried to hide it behind his back so I dove into the curve of his neck and planted a healthy hicky there.

"No fair. You play dirty," he grunted.

Right next to us my phone vibrated on the counter and he froze. "I thought we discussed how I don't like to share," he teased.

"It's not a client, it's Jesse. He's having trouble and I'm his knight in shiny armor."

"And he's having trouble with your *clients*." He backed away from me, a good-natured grin on his face and strawberries Romanov smeared all over his nice clothes.

Somehow, I'd managed to escape with food on my hands and face only.

"You're a mess." I swiped a bit of cream off his jacket and placed it in my mouth.

"Care to clean me up?" He leaned in to kiss the cream off my lips.

"As tempting as the offer sounds, I need to talk to Jesse in a bit. We have a trouble some client to handle."

"I see." He began to unbutton his shirt and I had to look away when he revealed the hard muscles underneath. "Are you sure?"

I turned around. "Go change, *Mr. Quinn*!"

He kissed the side of my neck. "I rather like it when you call me that. You'll have to do that more often when we're alone."

Xavier disappeared around a corner. The moment he was gone I tackled the phone call with Jesse. Apparently, a premier regatta was coming up in Boston and a client wanted to have a ladies' weekend on the bay during the boat races. Arrangements needed to made and I had to move the sun and moon to get them done. Poor Jesse. Most of the arrangements he could do, but he needed me to make a few key phone calls. Pull a string or two.

Compared to the mess on Xavier's shirt, a call or two was easy.

After I made the calls, I cleaned up our mess. Maid or not, I refused to be seen by his staff as untidy. A girl like me had an image to maintain.

By the time I finished cleaning, I was alone.

I drifted back to the sitting room. Immediately the crown caught my eye. I should've asked him who Rosalie was. None of the relatives at the compound had that name, but that didn't mean she might not be one.

And yet, the words etched on the crown wouldn't have come from an aunt or a cousin. The very meaning seemed intimate.

Instead of sitting the letting the crown bother me, I explored the rooms down the hall Xavier disappeared from. The house was silent, except for the faint sounds from my heels clicking on the mahogany hardwood floor. I took them off and left them along the wall. From the great room, I explored the rooms past the study into the hallway beyond.

The place seemed like a tomb. Far too quiet and lonely. After having noisy roommates for all these years, the very idea of living like this seemed unthinkable. I passed two locked doors. I came to a doorway that was cracked open.

Once inside, I could only see the shadows from what little light the moon leaked into the room. Compared to so many other rooms in the house, this particular room had shiny, bright disks all over the wall. The mystery to the disks was solved when I finally found the light switch. Countless medals, ribbons in cases covered the walls in another smaller study. Only a dark wooden desk and chair sat in the middle, but the walls were covered with countless things. First place, hurdles McCoy High School. Another one read first place 400 meter hurdles Blue Ridge High Invitational. So many other ones.

"Xavier Quinn, you've been holding back on me," I said with a small laugh. "You used to run track," I said with awe.

"Yeah, I had a personal coach who trained Olympic athletes and everything."

I turned around sharply to see him with wet hair. Sweat pants slung low on his narrow hips and a towel was draped over his shoulders.

Instead of letting him distract me, I continued to scan the wall. The dates kept going until ten years ago. Then everything came to a halt.

"These are amazing. How come you don't have any from college?" I asked.

"I didn't win any." He was following me. Hovering close enough to stir the butterflies dancing in my stomach.

"Is the scar on your knee from running?" All this time I'd been curious about the scar, but he'd seemed pretty tight-lipped about it after I'd asked.

Xavier sighed. "Yeah. Happened in college. It was one of my first meets of the year and I was running the 800-meter. There were a bunch of guys from the rival team who wanted to mess me up so they crowded me in during the first lap. Naturally, I tripped—"

"Ouch."

"But that wasn't the end of the story. I got back up."

We shared a smile. "I bet you caught up and won the whole thing," I said.

"Exactly."

Things grew quiet. He reached out and touched his knee. Countless times I'd run my hand down his legs, over his thighs. I'd brushed against the straight scar.

"During my fall, my right leg came down hard. I overextended my knee and tore every ligament you can imagine." He shrugged as if it was nothing, but I couldn't imagine what it would be like to train so hard, only to have to focus on something else. "I recovered, but after that no more scholarships. No more early morning practice."

While Xavier looked over one of his cases, his mind falling into the past, I noticed a lone image sitting in a frame on a desk. The frame was quite tiny, but the woman on the picture shined. Long blonde hair framed a stunning heart-shaped face. Her head was slightly turned as if she had been caught by surprise. Xavier sat beside her and he wasn't looking at the camera. His loving gaze rested on the woman beside him.

"Who's this?" I asked. "She's beautiful."

Xavier strolled over to me. "That's Rosalie."

"So she's the one who gave you the crown."

He only nodded, not glancing at me once. "Yeah, she's an old friend."

I swallowed the rude noise I wanted to make. "*An old friend?* Do you mean an old girlfriend?"

"Not anymore. She…passed away five years ago."

Heat filled my face. "I'm so sorry—"

"You didn't know. It's not a big deal."

But it was a big deal. No man kept an old girlfriend's custom gift or her picture unless he cared for her deeply. I felt so foolish. What his mother said earlier this evening during dinner echoed through my mind: *My son never brings his women here. The last time he did a few years ago, he thought it was funny to bring one of his playthings.*

No wonder he was so angry. He had loved Rosalie.

Maybe he still did.

Xavier walked to the doorway. He flicked off the light while I was still inside. "Are you coming?"

I left the room and its dark memories behind.

Chapter Twenty-Four

Xavier

"Most people love Saturdays," Sophie said as I drove us into Phoenix. "The sleeping in. The trips out and about. But, to be honest, I loathe weekends with a passion as powerful as a comb-over held down with crazy glue."

I chuckled. With such nice weather, I decided to take her out in my Bentley convertible. After finding her in the one place where I tried to bury and burn all my skeletons, the breeze and the open sky were welcomed.

"Everyone plans activities on the weekends. Before Jesse helped me, I worked the kind of hours that were subhuman. You wouldn't believe the kind of requests I've had." Sophie might've been venting, but she looked relaxed in a red sundress that ended on her upper thighs. Her gorgeous legs were stretched out. If she had any thoughts about finding Rosalie's picture, she kept them to herself.

"Condoms?" I tried.

"Oh, that's the kind of request the *nice* ones make."

"One guy wanted me to buy lingerie for his mistress—but he wanted me to *try* it on first."

"Seriously?"

"Yeah, I'd stretch out and destroy anything that's under size 4, but seriously I'd drop any man who wanted me to wear undies some other gal had tried on first." She shuddered at the thought. "This is a lesson for you. I like stuff that's brand new."

"Brand new," I echoed. Everything I had planned for Sophie would be top of the line and directly from the manufacturer. A few phone calls on the plane here from Boston had set everything in motion.

"So where are we going?" she asked.

"To see a painting." Ever since the opera, I'd wanted her to see the painting that reminded me of her. There was something about Sophie's profile that constantly ran through my mind every time I thought about it.

Our final destination was Phoenix Art Museum. As expected, Ian had made arrangements for our private showing.

"This should be fun." Her eyes brightened considerably.

The largest museum in the southwestern US beckoned us inside. I took her hand and we walked into the lobby to meet our guide.

"Good afternoon, Mr. Quinn," a young man, wearing a pin with the label Anatoly, said. "You're right on time."

"As always," Sophie quipped from beside me.

"Beauty never waits," I said.

Anatoly gave us a tour of the general exhibit, showing us pieces from Degas to Renoir. Sophie showed a bit of interest, but her face lightened up when Anatoly brought us to a private room. Chilled champagne had been left for us, along with the painting in particular I wanted her to see. Gustav Klimt's Water Serpents.

She passed the table and went straight to the painting. "Amazing. It's much smaller in person than I'd expected. After you told me about it, I looked it up online, but it's breathtaking up close. With those golden hues and lush backgrounds, those two women look ethereal."

I took her hand and drew her to the table. As expected, our tour guide had left us behind and closed the double doors to the room.

Then she looked at the closed doors. "Did he just leave us alone with a *priceless* painting?"

I poured two glasses for us. "I'm the one who paid for this museum to borrow it from the one in Austria. You could say I have an agreement with the foundation that countless lawyers have read and sighed."

"For one private viewing?" She tilted her head with a smile as I offered her a glass.

"For one viewing *with you*. I'd do anything for you, Sophie."

That made her blush. She turned toward the painting. "I don't know. The nymph at the top holding the other one is far prettier than me. She's got a fish's tail, too. Guys like that?"

I downed my champagne, enjoying the smooth, crisp flavor across my tongue. "I didn't say you looked exactly like her. You remind me of her."

She took a sip as I drew her in front of me. I wrapped my arms around her waist. Just feeling her close to me set me at ease. If I could keep holding her like this all day, I would. She leaned back and I placed against the strong pulse point at her neck. She was here in the present and I wanted to spend every moment with her until she agreed to stay with me.

We stared at the painting for a bit. Sophie must've grown restless though. Her right hand continued to hold her glass while her left reached behind her to run down my thigh. When she drew her hand behind her, she deftly brushed her hand near my hardening length. So teasingly close.

"Why does she remind you of me?" she breathed.

"Look at her face," I said close to her ear. "The parted lips. The eyes closed as if she's about to come."

"Maybe she's dreaming." She sucked in a breath when my hips pushed forward.

I ran my hands down her hips, then back up to her breasts. "Could be…Look at her breast. Klimt made it perfectly shaped. The nipple wonderfully pert." My fingertips drew circles over her nipples until they pebbled.

She moaned when I squeezed and kneaded her breasts. "I actually like The Kiss more than this one. Now that one was amazing."

I stopped to chuckle against her neck. "Forever the romantic."

I turned her around to capture her lips. Her kiss was slow. Deliberately sensual as she clutched me around the neck. My body came alive from her touch. I wanted her so badly. To feel her. To touch her. To make her mine so that she'd never consider leaving.

My hands gripped her ass, cupping and molding until she groaned into my mouth. She had to feel my need to be inside her rising higher.

She broke us apart to slyly grin at me. "You want me?" She was trying to sound serious and failed. "Right now? In front of this painting?"

I tugged her closer until her sundress hiked up and her legs wrapped around my waist. "Oh, hell, yes."

But instead of pulling her dress over her head and

bending her over the tiny table to take her hard and fast, my head dipped so that I could draw my lips across her pulse point. She shivered from my touch.

"Sophie," I murmured. Her thick hair smelled so good.

Our lips met again, the sensation delicious and dizzying in intensity.

"Please…" she whispered against my lips. That familiar begging that drove me wild. I kissed her lips again, determined to stretch out her pleasure. She loved to wait and I was willing to give her what she needed.

I drew my tongue across her lips. They were lush and sweet. Her mouth opened and my tongue brushed against hers. The pleasure was intense.

"Feel good?" I asked.

Our gazes locked and I watched her beautiful shudder. "Xavier."

Gently, I sat her down and we made quick work to discard each other's clothes. Shirts were tossed away to suck and flick at nipples. There were no gentle sucks from me this time. If she wouldn't wear my cuffs, I'd mark my territory in other ways—by briefly sucking hard on the soft, sensitive skin below her nipple.

Next her panties. I ripped those off so that I could fall to my knees to worship what lay between her thighs. She squirmed against me, clutching my hair while I nibbled and sucked on her clit. When she got close to coming, I backed off, only to come back again to taste her.

"When can you come?" I asked her.

"When you let me," she cried out.

A few hickies on her inner thighs would be sore reminders in the morning that I was the one who did this.

I was one who watched her back arch while she finally climaxed with my tongue spearing into her slick heat. She belonged to me and only me.

After I put on a condom, I was the one who shoved the champagne serving aside to bend her over the table. She gripped the table hard, looking back at me while I fucked her. The table shook with each thrust. Just watching her cry out was so hot. Awash in pleasure, all I could do was hold onto her while her pussy clenched my shaft. Sweet heaven, the pleasure was mind-numbing. A grumble formed in my chest, increasing in intensity as my balls hardened painfully.

"I'm coming, sweetheart," I grunted. My body stiffened, every nerve-ending in my cock exploding as reached my climax. It took me a bit of time to find my senses, but once I did, I continued to hold her in my arms. Each breath she took calmed me and reassured me she was here and if I didn't let her go she'd stay with me forever.

"You all right?" I asked her. She smiled at me and kissed my chin.

She looked at the champagne service on the floor and laughed. "That was…insane."

I drew my hands into her messy hair, pulling it back and out of her face. Her features had softened and her lips were bright and pink.

"Damn, you're so fucking beautiful," I whispered.

Instead of a joke to brush off my compliment, she averted her eyes and smiled.

Gently, I took her hand and kissed the palm, then the delectable skin at her pulse point. The skin thrummed there from her racing heart. Sato's wrist cuffs were gone now, but a part of me wanted her to wear the ones I gave her. Whether she wore them or not, it was Sophie I wanted. It was her I cared about.

"I have to go to the bathroom to freshen up. I'll be back." She put on her dress and left the room.

I found my clothes and got dressed. When Sophie

emerged from the bathroom, I followed her out to the lobby. Even though this outing went well, I sensed doubts swimming around that pretty head of hers.

My time was running out.

～

"ARE you sure you want to tangle with a pro like me?" I asked Sophie.

It was Sunday. My last day to show her how much I wanted her to stay with me.

We stood outside the Comfy Cow Ice Cream Shop, a place I used frequent as a student back in college at Arizona State University.

Back then, after every meet, I came here to face an adversary I never beat: The Fifteen Scoop Challenge.

A few athletes joined me in my quest, but naturally, the coaching staff wasn't aware of attempts to down a few days worth of calories in one shot.

At my side, Sophie's eyes shined with glee. "You're a pro at eating contests?"

"Not the contest, but the competition. I like to make wagers too," I said with grin. "If I win the challenge, you stay here with me, no questions asked—"

She gave a cute snort. "I stay if you win an eating contest? Is that the best you can do to convince me?"

Then she laughed, and I resisted the urge to kiss her lips, to pull her close to me. Like yesterday, she wore casual clothes again, a pair of jeans that revealed every curve and a blouse with an opening near her breasts that tempted me every time she sat next to me.

The fact that this weekend would come to an end soon bothered me constantly. Would we still be able to be together—like this—after she found out what I had planned for her?

Sophie led the way into the ice cream shop with a wry grin. Did she know something I didn't about the challenge? "Don't think just because we're eating a heavy lunch, that I'll carry you out of here."

I chuckled as I took in the place. So many memories here with old college friends. The Comfy Cow, with its rustic decor theme, had plenty of dark red seats for the busy student crowds when students filled the nearby Tempe campus. At this time of the year though, not as many students frequented campus so we could sit anywhere we wanted.

"Priceless paintings one day and an ice cream parlor the next. You're a worldly man, Mr. Quinn," she threw over her shoulder.

"There's so much more I'd love to show you." *So many more things, sweetheart.*

Sophie pointed out to the far wall with a bulletin board filled with Polaroid shots. "There's the *Wall of Shame* where your picture will be." She gestured to another wall with a board labeled *Victory Lane.* "And that's where my lovely photo will be displayed for posterity. May the Ashton name live on."

I held in a laugh. *She had no idea that my photo was already there...* "In infamy for overeating?"

She shoved my shoulder for good measure.

At the ordering counter, she asked for two helpings of the Fifteen Scoop Challenge. Casually, I took her hand after she ordered. Her fingers intertwined with mine and the warmth from her palm spread through me. A man could get used to this pleasant feeling.

"Don't think you can distract me from winning," she whispered. "I have nerves made of Rocky Road."

I took in the types of ice cream, sensing that she wasn't facing me, yet our hands continued to stay connected. After the manager set everything up, we sat down at one of the tables.

"The rules are simple folks," the manager explained. "You get one hour to eat fifteen scoops of ice cream covered in whipped cream, nuts, and sauces."

While the manager continued to speak, I patted my flat belly. Even back when I was in college, that huge bowl of ice cream had been intimidating, but one look at Sophie's face, and I knew a poker face was essential to winning this game. I'd show her how driven I was for her to stay.

"The winner gets a T-shirt and a free meal. The loser gets to pay for everything."

We both nodded. Sophie pointed two fingers at her eyes and then gestured to mine. She could watch me all she wanted. Cheating this particular contest would be near to impossible unless I was hiding a refrigerated container somewhere.

The countdown started and then we were off. I tackled the ice cream first. 'Cause I had a plan: eat the firmer ice cream and then inhale the whipped cream closer to the end. The cherries disappeared quickly as well as the spoonfuls of nuts sprinkled on top. Not long into the challenge, I'd experienced more episodes of brain freeze than I'd ever had in his life.

"I can tell you're getting full," Sophie said with a mouthful of strawberry. "Just give up now and I'll be merciful."

As the end of the hour drew closer, our pace had slowed considerably. Her lack of enthusiasm concerned me.

"If you're not having fun anymore, we should stop. Before you get sick," I managed.

"Are you just looking for an out? If you're feeling ill, I understand." She was trying to be strong and all, but I could tell she was too full to eat more.

"I'm done." I put the spoon down, my stomach heavy with food. "Come take my loser picture."

Sophie cheered her victory, not an enthusiastic one, but a cheer nonetheless. "I'm going to fall over and get rolled out of here by the staff."

I was rather full myself. Sophie continued to recover while I slowly stood and paid for the ice cream.

Instead of heading to the car, we kept walking along the sidewalk into campus, enjoying the cool weather brought on by sunset.

"You want to keep going?" I asked her. Hopefully, she said yes. There were a few things she needed to see.

"Yeah," she murmured. "I need to walk this off."

The Arizona State University campus extended for several miles, but our destination wasn't too far from here. As we weaved around on the paths between buildings, she threw a questioning glance or two in my direction, but didn't say anything until we reached the Cornerstone Business Research Facility.

"What's this place?" she asked.

"An incubator for startups on campus. They provide facilities for businesses."

She nodded. "So what are we doing here?"

I took her hand and drew her through the double doors. "You'll see."

The receptionist waiting behind a counter smiled at us. "Good afternoon, Mr. Quinn. It's a pleasure to see you again."

I nodded her way and directed Sophie to the elevators.

"Seems like you're important around here. The receptionist in my building at Cambridge doesn't even acknowledge my presence half the time."

I shrugged. "You could say I'm recent donor."

That made her go 'ah' for a bit.

From the fifth floor, we headed down a narrow hallway to many closed doors. The signs had names of companies I'd never heard of, but the vibe was one that I was quite familiar with. Silver Sparrow Systems started out in a place like this. Just a bunch of people sitting in a small room pounding away at keyboards, hoping and praying venture capitalists would invest in the ideas we generated. I happen to be one of the lucky ones.

At the end of the hallway, we came to a set of double doors.

"There's no sign," Sophie remarked.

"I know." I pulled a keycard from my back pocket and brushed the card against the reader attached to the door. After an audible click, the door unlocked.

As she walked into the huge office suite, I waited for her smile—any type of reaction to show she was pleased, but I got silence.

She scanned the modern lavender-colored couches near door to the receptionist desk. From beyond there, she wandered into the private office in the back.

The silence was killing me. She walked into the private office bathroom, briefly flicking the light on and off.

At first, I expected her to ask what all this was, but Sophie was far sharper than the women I'd dated in the past.

"This was unexpected," she began.

"Too much?" When I'd made the arrangements I thought it was too little. Hiring for secretary could begin as soon as Monday.

"This is the perfect place for you to start again. Many

of the companies here will need insight and assistance from someone with your level of experience." I kept going as she approached the windows, adding distance between us both physically and mentally. "I also began to make arrangements for you to meet with local CEOs—"

"Xavier…"

I still kept going until she bit out, "Just don't."

Silence stood between us, stealing the words I wanted to say. I wanted to tell her I'd take care of her, but she didn't want to hear that. Everything we'd done today—all the fun we'd had—and I couldn't give her the one thing she truly wanted: Success.

"I'm going to London," she finally said.

Everything in me hardened and a familiar feeling came over me: utter disappointment.

"Why?" I hadn't meant for my reply to come out so harshly, but it did. "I said I'd—"

"You said you'd take care of me. I don't want that. I've been on my own since I was eighteen." She looked at me briefly, but when I looked back at her with the upset I couldn't hide she looked away. "Just like you, I have aspirations. I have things I'm relentless about accomplishing and my career is one of them. I don't want to start off at square one again."

"You'd be starting fresh in London."

"I would be working with Carlie's clients and supporting her when she needs me."

"Then I could *get* you clients."

"I know you could, but I don't want that." She touched me briefly and I wanted to hold her hand against my heart. My damn heart hurt. "Say I moved to London? Would we be happy if we lived like that? Seeing each other every couple of months?"

No, I wouldn't be happy with that. I wanted her with me all the time. By my side. In my bed.

As I strode toward her, filling the gap she'd created, I wondered if something more was at play. When I reached her side, she still didn't look at me. "Is it just your job, or maybe you haven't let Sato go? Have you opened up enough to accept being with me?"

She jerked back and showed her wrist. "I've already said my final goodbyes and moved on."

Just seeing her bare skin burned me. What I wouldn't give to see her wearing my cuffs. To know that she had bound herself to me the way I was bound to her. "So why not wear mine then?"

"Because…" she bit out. "I can't tie myself to someone I have to let go." She marched back the way we came.

"Don't go like this." I followed her and grabbed her arm. She wasn't walking out on me yet. "Why can't you give in on this *one thing*?" I growled. "We can make it work if stop running away and love me like I love you."

"I'm running where I need to be. If we end it now, no one has to *leave* before things get serious." She closed her eyes so tightly as if in pain. "If we end it now, no one gets hurt."

That stopped me cold. *When someone you love leaves it always hurts whether it's sooner or later.*

Briefly, she bit her lip as if she hadn't meant to let those words slip out.

"I'd never leave you, Sophie," I said firmly, meaning every word. "I want you to stay with me."

"You told me from the beginning you didn't want a relationship. I heard you and I respected that."

"Yeah, I used to feel that way, but not anymore." Frustration made it harder for me think.

"Look at your life and your accomplishments. What has ultimately made you happy?" she asked.

Every time I walked into my office at Silver Sparrow I answered that question: conquering what fell into my path. Every failure made my successes all the sweeter. Denying her happiness for my own selfish reasons was something I'd never do to her. Not in the way it had been done to me. I loved her too much to see her questioning her decision to stay.

When I finally spoke, it was done deal. "If you want to go, I won't stand in your way. I'll have the jet ready to take you back home."

Chapter Twenty-Five

Sophie

Packing, whether you want to go to the destination or not, still bites. Case in point, I couldn't seem to pack my belongings back in Boston without breaking something. A beautiful tiger's eye vase from Thailand ended up in enough pieces to create a mosaic. Four CDs, yep I still had those, turned into scratched up coasters when Lana accidentally stepped on a few.

I packed away all my cookbooks. They were coming with me, but all my Japanese language-learning materials were shipped as a donation to a library in NYC. Holding onto them when I didn't study anymore seemed wasteful.

No matter how many disasters came my way, my empty room even seemed like a reminder of what I was letting go. In the spot where my bed had sat, Xavier had made love to me. In another corner, right next to my desk, he'd placed a beautiful red box in my hand. What I wouldn't give right now for him to be standing here.

But the room was empty and I had nothing but regrets to fill it.

Getting excited about spending time with Carlie wasn't the same as it used to be.

What about the good days? Like the days we used what little money we had to enjoy ice cream cones at Eddies Sweet Shop?

I cracked a grin at the sunny feeling such a moment washed over me. Those had been good times. We had a few of them—but we were older now with our own aspirations.

Living in the UK with her would be different now.

You wouldn't have him, I reminded myself. I wouldn't see Penny or Griffin as often either, but I'd have Carlie and I owed it to her.

Broken discs and all.

I barely heard the doorbell ring.

Immediately, my breath quickened with a single thought: Had Xavier come back for me?

Before Lana had a chance to reach the door, I was there peeking through the peephole, ready to see his face.

I saw a familiar blonde with a smirk instead.

"Carlie?" I gasped.

I opened the door and she giggled when she saw my surprised face.

"Hey, Sophie." She snuck in a hug and then looked around for a place to sit. "I'm taking the red eye next time." She collapsed on the couch and Lana gave me a wave before she slinked back to her bedroom.

"W-what are you doing here?" I stammered.

She crossed her legs, revealing her expensive Louboutins. "Personal business."

That personal business must be her parents.

"So where are your bags?" I asked.

"At my hotel, of course. Just seeing the surprised look on your face was worth every fee I've paid!" She giggled mischievously.

I took a place next to her on the couch. "You still haven't answered my question."

She took my hand and played with the silver rings on my fingers. "It's time for me settle my personal business."

"For how long? I'm about to move to London. I'll need—"

"Plans have changed." The look she gave me was dead serious.

"Carlie." Utter disbelief had me shaking my head. "You've thrown me for a loop a few times, but today's surprise is beyond messed up. It's borderline *fucked* up."

She let go of my hand. "What's messed up is how you left behind Xavier for me."

"You're my best friend. My family. We take care of each other."

She smiled at me. "That's what I'm doing right now, Sophie. I'm taking care of you. You're staying here. You're going to unpack your fucking bags and get back together with him."

I rested my head against her shoulder, flabbergasted at what just occurred. "That's not possible."

"Why the hell not?"

"He's in Arizona now. More importantly, he wanted to give me the world and I want to conquer it myself." I gave a half-shrug. "As lonely as I've been feeling over the last month, I've been regretting my decision to leave. At the time, it seemed like the best thing to do since I was moving." Over the weeks I continued to rationalize what I'd done, but the part of me that felt carved out and empty seemed to grow emptier.

"Then call him after I leave and figure things out." She

gave me another look. The one where her sharp blonde eyebrows lowered and her olive green eyes darkened.

How many times had I checked the contacts on my phone? Countless times I'd browsed his profile. My feet wouldn't fight me to walk over to my cellphone, but my heart refused such an action. What if he didn't want me back? I'd refused him.

She touched my bare wrist as if to further make a point. "I see you threw away those damn leather cuffs from Sato."

"It was time. A long time ago."

"He never collared you. If I would've had my way, I would've cut that shit into strips and watched how fast they burned in a garbage can on the curb."

A laugh jumped out of me. "Say what you're *really* thinking, Car."

She rolled her eyes. "That was the tame version of what I was thinking."

I made us two cups of English Grey and we sat together for a while, chatting about what I'd seen and experienced in Phoenix. I'd glossed over the details with my roommates, but Carlie got everything. For a brief moment, I felt like we were back in that minuscule Queens apartment sharing our experiences—both the good and the bad.

By the time I gushed about the ice cream-eating contest, she was smiling on the outside, but I could tell she was pained. I'd seen this look before. As hard as she was trying to hide it, I could see her discomfort simmering under the surface of her skin.

"You're going to see him," I said to her.

She didn't say yes or no. No nod or anything. "It's just for one drink," she murmured.

"You two are like a metronome. Back and forth. One

knocking the other off kilter. Only to later have the same thing reciprocated."

"It won't be the same this time. We're meeting once. That's it."

I snorted. "That's what you think each and every time."

"He's the one who found the information about my parents."

"You don't owe him a damn thing. You two can't make it work!"

"It's complicated, Sophie."

Wow, seemed pretty crystal clear to me after she came home crying for weeks all those years ago. "Bullshit."

She glanced at the pink watch on her wrist. "My time is up."

"How convenient."

Her lips formed a straight line. "Don't be like this. Not right now when I need you."

"I've seen the aftermath—that's all. It's not pretty."

She pulled me into a hug and I held her close.

Before she left, she whispered, "Before the aftermath, it was beautiful though."

Chapter Twenty-Six

Xavier

Today was a day to celebrate. After two months worth of negotiations, Silver Sparrow Systems had a contract with Nakamura's company for the use of their facilities. Research and development.

I couldn't stop thinking about her.

This morning Ian was haggling me about the trip to Japan to meet with the development team. Ian had packed my bags and made all the arrangements, but I hadn't left Phoenix and had I no plans to do so.

Sophie wouldn't let you drag your feet like this.

No, she wouldn't. She would've found a way to manipulate me so I showed up at the airport. The minute I got on that jet though, I would be adding thousands of miles between us.

Instead of dwelling on the issue, I went through my business for the day. My first email was from Ian. A property I put up for sale had sold quickly. The next one made me smile. My Director of Operations planned to offer a bonus to everyone. As much as I tried to be excited for my staff, I continued to stare outside of the window from my office out to the desert. I took in the rocky landscaping, somehow expecting to see the bay, to feel salty breeze from the ocean.

My phone weighed heavy in my pocket.

Instead of staring out the window, I sent a single text message to Marcus: *Meet me at the creek.*

I waited for him to text me back and complain about how I needed to go to Japan, but I got back a quick, 'k', instead.

By the time I got to the compound, Marcus was waiting for me out at the creek. The place couldn't be called such anymore. The creek had dried up before we'd been born. My uncle talked about how he'd swam in the water as a kid with my dad, but I couldn't imagine this place in any other matter.

All you could do now was sit at the end of the dock and contemplate things that were lost and would never come back.

"Want a beer?" Marcus asked me.

"Naw, I'm good."

I didn't want alcohol to dull my senses. I was in pain and I accepted it.

"How you been holding up?" I asked. "Becca recovering all right?"

"Yeah, she's sleeping off the last chemo session."

I nodded. "You don't have to worry about anything. I've got it all covered."

Marcus patted my shoulder. "I know you do."

The need to swing my legs was almost automatic, but I didn't.

"So what's on your mind? Aren't you supposed to be on a plane in a few hours?" Marcus asked.

I took a deep breath. "I need you to tell me to leave."

Marcus chuckled. "You want me to tell you to forget about her like Rosalie—you know you're the smartest guy I know, but right now I feel like you're stupid as fuck."

I threw a dark glance in his direction. Marcus rarely talked to me this way.

"For the first time ever, you bring a girl home I can see you're serious about and you just let her go."

"She doesn't want me. Not in the way I want her." And I needed to let her go somehow.

"Are you sure about that?" Marcus asked.

"She left, didn't she?"

Marcus chuckled. "I think you forgotten how bad ass you can be. Look, I know a good woman when I see one, Xav. Get in that plane and *fly* to the UK if you have to."

"It's not that simple." Nothing in life ever was.

"Do you love her?"

I immediately nodded.

"Then don't let her go. What the hell are you doing here?"

He did have a point there.

~

I PACKED my bags not long after I got back to the house. The place seemed cavernous, practically empty when everyone wasn't gathered together. This was how I grew up and I still didn't like it nowadays. That's why I had my own place closer to Phoenix.

One thing I couldn't do though before leaving was saying goodbye to mom. If I was going after Sophie—and I wasn't coming back without here—Mom needed to know what I planned to do.

She wouldn't disrespect Sophie again no matter how resentful she felt to me.

I found her in the sitting room reading a book.

"Hey, Mom," I said.

She didn't look up. "Xavier, I thought you left for the day."

"I did. I'm about to go back to the east coast." I sat down directly in front of her and she looked up immediately.

"What about the company?"

"I'm not leaving for a long time. I'm going back to take care of some business."

"The girl."

I smiled. "Did Marcus call you?" They talked on the phone all the time. As much as I tried not to be jealous, sometimes I got that way.

"No, he didn't this time. I might be your mom, but I'm also a woman who walked away from the man who loved her."

My eyebrow rose. "Dad always said you two had the perfect engagement and everything."

She placed her book in her lap. Thinking about dad always made her smile and the bitterness melted away a bit. "I sabotaged our relationship at every opportunity. Back when I was dating, most men would end everything before it began. I was never good-looking."

"Oh, stop it, you're gorgeous."

She rolled her eyes. "You're a good son, but even I knew that most men never treated me well. I was forced to live in the moment."

Like my beautiful Sophie.

She continued. "After dating your father for a year, I left Phoenix for Georgetown. I'd never been with a man for so long."

"And he went after you."

"August Quinn didn't build companies only to have the woman he wanted walk away." She looked at me as if she examined me. "You and your dad are alike in so many ways. Driven to success, but blind to matters of the heart."

"That I agree."

"I can't keep you from going, you're a Quinn after all, but I just don't want you going into something you're not prepared for."

"I'm prepared to be happy. I've wanted to be happy even after you and dad abandoned me after I stopped running. It was a lot harder without you."

She looked away, her hands tightening on her book.

We'd walked into unknown territory. This particular conversation never had happened unfortunately.

"Things never should have gone that way," she admitted. "I have regrets."

We were quiet for a while; the only sound in the room came from the hum of the air conditioning coming through the vents. The light sound of tick tock from the clock on the wall.

I stood there for a bit, waiting, hoping.

Then she finally spoke. "Moving on is hard, you know," she said gently.

The sigh I released was a heavy one. "Yes, it is. The past is dragging us down and even I will admit it's time for me to move on."

I turned to leave, but not without saying goodbye. A bridge had been built today between my mother and me. The structure wasn't steady, but perhaps someday it would be.

Chapter Twenty-Seven

Sophie

Another day, another irate diva. Did I tell you that weekends have become my least favorite time of the week? My weekend with Xavier had made up for that particular thought a bit, but as of right now, I wanted to jump into the bay and see how far I'd get to the UK. Even if Carlie wasn't there.

"Miss Ashton," my customer Pearl Donahue began, "I thought when I hired you, you'd be on top of things for my friends. All this waiting is boresome." Pearl, who was fifty-six going on twenty-nine based on the clothes she *didn't* have on, quirked a smile and adjusted her five thousand dollar sunglasses from Milan.

How did I know the price for those suckers? I made sure a pair was available for five ladies at the crack of dawn on the Donahue yacht. As well as gift baskets containing expensive soaps made of goat's milk from Sweden.

"Now, now, Miss Donahue." Jesse returned to the deck

to meet us. He stood next to her spot on her deck chair and patted her shoulder. She giggled uncontrollably. "I spoke with the Captain and he said all the traffic from the regatta has made leaving the marina difficult." His words were smooth with Southern silk.

"I told you, sweetheart." Pearl turned to him with appreciation, batting her eyes with massive eyelash extensions that resembled little wiggling spider legs. "Call me Pearl."

Pearl? She'd been Miss Donahue to me since I made the arrangements for a girls' weekend in Boston for the America's Cup. The city was buzzing with the regatta going on right now. The America's Cup hadn't been here for the past five years, so the who's who in the Boston celebrity circle could be seen partying on other yachts close by. It took Jesse and I over an hour to reach the Donahue yacht.

As much as I enjoyed the festive mood around me, a part of me wished I were relaxing in a hotel suite off the bay watching the events with someone in particular.

"Don't you agree, Miss Ashton?" someone from my left, one of Pearl's companion's, asked me. "Boston was so overdue for a regatta."

I shoved my moment of reverie overboard to smile at one of Pearl's guests. "Of course. Valencia is nice and all, but there's something special about the Bay."

Yep, there was something special about the Bay. Briefly, I thought about eating fish tacos with Xavier. With his competitive spirit, he'd like seeing this scene with all these well-crafted sail boats with large corporate logos.

"Speaking of Spain," Pearl's friend mentioned, "this fall Pearl, you should come to Porto Cervo with Carl and me. We'll be spending the summer there while the kids enjoy Brussels."

I kept smiling, not having the heart to remind her Sardinia was in Italy...

"If I have someone to enjoy the trip with, I might do that." Pearl took in Jesse's ass while he spoke with someone on the phone—most likely the caterer she flew in from Miami. As Jesse's employer I was horrified. As nice as his ass was, I was drawing the line if she grabbed it. Before my mouth opened to shift the cougar club meeting's attention elsewhere, one of the skippers from below crossed the expansive deck and approached me. "Are you Sophie Ashton?" he asked.

I nodded. "Is something the matter?" *Smile until your cheeks go numb, Sophie.*

"We have a boat off the stern that has requested your presence."

"*Excuse me?*" From where we stood, with the tallest part of the yacht in the way, I couldn't see anything behind us.

After excusing myself, I followed the skipper around the side of the ship. As another yacht, a bit bigger, came into view, my heartbeat began to quicken, along with my steps. Soon enough, I passed the skipper, practically running up to the back of the boat to see the most beautiful sight.

Across the deck of the other boat was a sea of moon flowers. Beautiful white and pink flowers swaying with the ocean's breeze.

And there he stood in the middle of them, waiting for me.

The skipper had caught up to me and he had a wry grin on his face. "I assumed you'd want to see this."

"I hope it's for me. Would be awkward otherwise," I murmured.

Xavier and I stared at each other for a bit, before the

skipper tapped my shoulder. "Unless you plan to fly over there, Mr. Quinn has a boat waiting to take you there."

I nodded. While I headed over there I sent Jesse a quick message: *"Heading to see someone very special. Take good care of Miss Donahue. Keep your clothes on, please."*

The small boat couldn't take me to see him fast enough. My whole body sang with excitement then as we approached the back of his boat where I could board, fear and doubt crept up my spine. He'd finally come to see me, but what did he want this time. What demands would he make to upend my life?

Wave after wave of the wonderful scent flowed through my nostrils. The whole place was like heaven. I reached out and touched a few. As expected their petals were closed. Their time to bloom was coming soon.

As much as I wanted to put my arms around him, I kept my distance.

"Xavier." For a couple of breaths we stared at each other. "What are you...?" I knew the obvious answer, but I wanted to hear his answer.

"I came for you."

I briefly closed my eyes. Even though he was standing a few feet away, I could feel him. The breeze brought his scent to me, too and my body immediately responded in kind.

But I didn't know what to say.

He reached out to brush his fingertips against mine. "I'm not leaving until you agree to be with me."

Then he glanced down and saw the hand he'd brushed against. "You're wearing them."

He ran his hand over the brand new leather cuffs I wore. *His* leather cuffs.

"Yes." I wore his heart on me now—even before my little talk with Carlie. I had been for a while now.

Nervously, I shifted from one foot to another.

"I sold my building in Phoenix," he finally said.

"Why?" He'd spent so much time on making it a home.

"I did some thinking. It's just a place to lay my head. I had to let it go if I wanted to start fresh with you."

I only nodded.

"I'm glad you didn't leave," he added.

"But I left you and I said no to *us* too. I distinctly remember you saying you never take no for an answer unless there is a *good* reason. There must've been a *very good* reason back then. So why now?" I asked.

I had to know. Missing me wasn't good enough.

"I always work to get what I want so that I hear yes." He closed the gap even more. I wanted him to touch so badly. "I wanted you to be happy and I didn't want to be the one to hold you back. I let you go because I love you, Ashley."

Every time he used that name I came undone.

"So what are you saying?" I crossed my arms, pleased to hear he wanted me to carve out my own destiny, but why should I stay with him?

He quirked a grin that made my stomach flutter. His lips parted a bit. "I'm saying I'm not taking no for an answer this time unless you have a damn good enough reason why we shouldn't be together. You're not going to London and I'm willing to make things work—no matter the distance."

I took in the perfect blue sky and chewed on what I could say back. He waited for my reasons, but whatever I threw at him, he'd cast them all aside. Maybe that's because I didn't have any reasons to say no. Finally, I spoke.

"I always make sure my clients are satisfied," I said quietly.

"I'm not a client anymore." He closed in, effectually blocking my path back the way I'd come from. It was all or nothing time.

"No, you're not." I held in a groan. "You can't be right all the time, but in this particular instance, I've tried to think of something and I can't."

He drew me close until our lips brushed. Having his arms around me felt right. Felt perfect. "Then stay with me tonight. Stay with me forever, Sophie." He tilted his head toward the flowers. "There will be quite the show tonight when these beauties bloom."

"I like this plan," I agreed. "I do my best work in the moonlight."

His dark smile left me without a doubt that I'd made the best decision. "Indeed, you do."

Epilogue

Sophie

For the entire weekend, we lived on Xavier's boat. I have to admit experiencing the Regatta as an observer, and not as someone's employee, was a delight.

Months passed. Winter swept into Boston. As he'd promised, Xavier never helped me. Not a single dime. What he did offer though was encouragement and love. When he did offer advice though, I listened. Who in their right mind turned down advice from a billionaire?

What I did concede to was living together—when he spent his weekends in Boston or when he telecommuted. We made a new home together in downtown Boston on the top floor of the very building where I made him stay in that tiny studio apartment. *Go figure.*

After a long day of working I came home to an empty apartment and a handwritten note from Xavier on the end table next to the front door.

The insatiable Mr. Quinn strikes again. A new note meant a new game to play.

I couldn't stop smiling while I read: *Get in the elevator and go down to the studio apartment on the fourth floor. Take off your clothes, blindfold yourself, and get into the bed.*

He wanted me to go back to the studio apartment. Very nice.

After such a crazy day in the wintry weather, my feet hurt and the possibility of a hot bath beckoned me, but I complied. I knew very well what was coming so I did as I was told and Xavier knew I loved an order I couldn't refuse.

So I made the trip down to the studio apartment. The place was pitch black and the air was stuffy. I peered into the shadows. Was he waiting in the shadows for me? I left my sweater dress on staircase. My garters on the dresser next to the bed. I placed my bra and panties at the foot of the bed.

Then I used the blindfold on the bed to cover my eyes.

I waited and waited in the cold apartment.

The chill in the room brushed against my skin, but I didn't so much as twitch.

By the time I shivered, I sensed someone approaching. He made me wait even longer, and all I could do was imagine his gaze caressing me in the darkness. He finally brushed his fingertips against my core. The briefest of touches. Teasing me was his specialty at this point and he pleased me every single time.

He always came for me and I always accepted him.

I shifted my hand to reach for him.

"I warned you, Sophie," he whispered, his breath close to my mouth. He was so teasingly close to kissing me.

He continued. "Now, you'll be punished."

"Please touch me tonight," I wanted to whisper. What

would the punishment be today? Instead of letting me anticipate more pleasure, he rolled me over onto my stomach and gave my ass a gentle smack. The sound bounced off the walls and I had to hold in a moan. He ran his fingertip down the middle of back, along the seam of my ass to the placed where I wanted him the most. From there, he fondled my buttocks before giving me a hard slap on each cheek.

I gasped from the searing warmth spreading along my butt cheeks. He could do that to me again and again until I was begging.

"You're so beautiful like this," he said as he pressed his chest to my back. "My beautiful, love." He was on top of me now. I felt everything, yet I couldn't turn around to wrap my arms around him and tell him I felt the same. His shaft rested against the back of my thigh. Hard and ready.

I was his and he was mine.

"What should I do to you tonight?" he whispered. His thick finger circled my tight opening, slipping into the indentation and slipping back out. My stomach quaked, and I pushed back against his finger.

Quicker than I expected him to react, he grabbed a fistful of my hair with one hand and pulled my hips upward with the other. I gasped as he thrust deep inside of me.

"I prefer this for now." The bed groaned from the force of his thrusts. Over and over again he showed me how much he desired me. How much he refused to let me go. I took all the love he offered. He knew exactly what I wanted. Tension gathered around my scalp where he gripped my hair. Again and again he filled me until I screamed my release.

He rolled me over and gently pulled the blindfold off. "Hello, Ashley."

A name I used to hate hearing filled me with joy every time he said it.

"Hey…love." Did he really expect me to reply as he continued to pleasure me to the point where my toes curled and my back arch.

Just watching him watch me made it harder. Every caress, every kiss, sent me spiraling higher.

With a grunt, his back straightened. I watched him bite his lip. His climax blossomed inside of me as his love always did.

Once our quickened breathes slowed, he kissed my forehead. "So what if I told you I wanted to relocate to Boston permanently?"

I couldn't hide my smile. "I'd like that."

"And what if I wanted to marry you, too?" He kissed my nose and my mouth dropped.

"You're not very good at proposing," I blurted. "Or giving gifts."

He laughed. "I just said I want to spend the rest of my life with you and you're chastising my approach?"

"Pretty much."

"So what do you say?" He reached over to the drawer next to the bed and pulled a box from inside. A ring-shaped box.

I took a deep breath. I couldn't believe this was happening. "Yes, Xavier, I'll marry you."

He placed the massive princess-cut diamond ring on my finger. "I'm glad you said yes this time."

I snorted, thinking of when he offered me the cuffs. "You did it right this time."

"Are you upset I didn't make you wait long for a proposal?"

I ran my fingers along his chin, reveling in the feel of

his stubble. "Not at all. I've waited long enough to find you."

"Was I worth the wait?"

"You'll have to put in the work to show me whether you're worth it, Mr. Quinn. I'm thinking countless hours of rope work. Maybe even a trick or two with a riding crop."

He ran his fingers down my legs again, grinning like a wolf about to pounce his prey. "Ashley, I'd be delighted to show you again and again."

surrender to you

AT YOUR SERVICE   BOOK 2

ARE YOU READY FOR
CARLIE JASON'S STORY?

About the Author

Shawntelle Madison is a Web developer who loves to weave words as well as code. She'd be reluctant to admit it, but if pressed, she'd say that she covets and collects source code. After losing her first summer job detasseling corn, Madison performed various jobs, from fast-food clerk to grunt programmer to university webmaster. Writing eccentric characters is her favorite job of all. On any given day when she's not surgically attached to her computer, she can be found watching cheesy horror movies or the latest action-packed anime. Shawntelle Madison lives in Missouri with her husband and children.